The Ice Diamond Quest

Other books by Eric Wilson

The Tom and Liz Austen Mysteries

1. Murder on *The Canadian*
2. Vancouver Nightmare
3. The Ghost of Lunenburg Manor
4. Disneyland Hostage
5. The Kootenay Kidnapper
6. Vampires of Ottawa
7. Spirit in the Rainforest
8. The Green Gables Detectives
9. Code Red at the Supermall
10. Cold Midnight in Vieux Quebec

Also available by Eric Wilson

Summer of Discovery
The Unmasking of 'Ksan

The Ice Diamond Quest

A Tom and Liz Austen Mystery

by

Eric Wilson

HarperCollins*PublishersLtd*
Toronto

The author describes many real places and events in this book, but the story and the characters come entirely from his imagination.

First published in 1990
by HarperCollins Publishers Ltd.
Suite 2900, Hazelton Lanes
55 Avenue Road
Toronto, Ontario, M5R 3L2

Canadian Cataloguing in Publication Data

Wilson, Eric
  The ice diamond quest

ISBN 0-00-223589-7

I. Title.

PS8595.I4793128 1990 jC813'.54 C90-094828-0
PZ7.W55Ic 1990

Printed and bound in Canada by
T. H. Best Printing Co. Ltd.

For three special friends
Eve, Peg and Phoebe

1

The man in the creased leather jacket stared at Tom
Austen.

"What's that you just said kid? About an Ice Diamond?"

Tom pretended not to hear. He was in a jet approaching the airport at St. John's, the capital city of
Newfoundland. His sister Liz was beside the window; the
man sat to Tom's right. He was about 30, and smelled of
cigarettes. His fingers were yellow with nicotine; he
wore a black t-shirt, jeans and battered boots. On his
head was a cowboy hat, stained by long use.

The man grabbed Tom's arm. "Pay attention when I'm
talking to you, kid. You just said something to that girl

about an Ice Diamond. I want to know why."

Across the aisle, a woman with red hair and blue eyes looked toward them. "Is there a problem, Tom?"

He shook his head. "It's okay, Mom."

The man glanced tensely at Mrs. Austen. Then he dropped his grip on Tom and leaned back in his seat, closing his eyes. Tom smiled at his mother — who was sitting apart from them because she'd made last-minute reservations — and then he looked out the window.

As the jet banked over the city, he saw the golden light of the setting sun reflected from the harbour, which was almost enclosed by cliffs. Spread over the hills of the city was a spiderweb of streets with houses painted many bright colours. At the narrow harbour opening waves smashed against the cliffs, throwing white water high in the air.

"I'm looking for Deadman's Hill," Tom said to his sister. "In the old days they'd hang the bodies of convicted murderers there for sailors to see as their ships entered the harbour."

"That's so gross. Whatever for?"

"To warn against causing trouble while they were in port. I bet it worked." Tom leaned closer to the window. "Down there Marconi received the first audio signal from across the Atlantic. I wonder if it was a coded message for a spy?"

Liz smiled. She had on new jeans and a blazer over a white blouse, and wore a patterned band in her gleaming dark hair; her new watch, a gift from her Dad, was already set on Newfoundland time. "I can't believe we were packing our suitcases this morning in Winnipeg, and now we're looking down at the Atlantic."

"Flying still makes you nervous?" Tom said.

"Of course not!"

He smiled. "Then why are you clutching that combination four-leaf clover and rabbit's foot?"

"Because you gave it to me, and I always travel with it."

"Mom says we visited Newfoundland when we were tiny kids. Do you remember anything about it?"

Liz shook her head. "I was three years old, and you were one. Mom says it was wonderful going home to Newfoundland, to show off her babies to all her relatives."

"Too bad it's such a sad occasion that's bringing us back now." Tom glanced across the aisle. "Mom's doing okay so far. But it'll be tough when we go to the hospital to visit Nanny."

"I can't believe our grandmother's dying. She was in such great spirits the last time she visited us."

"Sure, but that was two years ago."

Liz nodded. "You're right."

Tom tightened his seat belt as the airport came into view, then the wheels touched down. Mrs. Austen looked at Tom and Liz as they left the plane. "I feel so sad about Nanny, but it's good to be home."

"I'm glad we're with you," Tom said, and Liz nodded her agreement.

At the end of an enclosed ramp they entered the terminal. "By the way, Tom," Mrs. Austen said, "what was the problem with that cowboy on the plane?"

"I'm not sure, Mom. Remember I received a letter from our cousin Duncan, just before we left home? I was talking to Liz about the letter when that man grabbed me."

"What did Duncan say in his letter?"

"He's really excited to meet us, so he can't wait for our arrival in Petty Harbour. Where exactly is your home town, Mom?"

"Down the coast, south of St. John's. Petty Harbour's

a fishing village that faces the open Atlantic."

"Duncan said he went up on a hill above Petty Harbour with his old-fashioned spyglass towards dark one evening recently. He was checking out the Atlantic when he spotted a luxury yacht approaching. It stopped off-shore, and began flashing a signal."

"Could Duncan understand the signal?" Mrs. Austen asked.

Tom shook his head. "He's only 10, so he hasn't had a chance to study signalling yet. But he wrote down the pattern of long and short flashes, then tried to figure out the message using a book on signalling. He's pretty sure the message was about an Ice Diamond."

"What happened to the yacht?"

"It sailed away. But Duncan saw it another evening, repeating the signal, and he's sure it'll return again. He's hoping we'll get to Petty Harbour in time to see it ourselves."

"If the yacht returns," Liz said, "we'll be able to help Duncan work out the signal."

Tom nodded. "Maybe then we'll understand why that cowboy got so interested when Liz and I were talking about the Ice Diamond."

Mrs. Austen shook her head. "You kids attract mysteries like you're magnets."

"Don't worry about us, Mom. We'll be fine."

"Let's hope so. I've got enough on my mind with Nanny so ill, and your Dad off in Arizona helping their police look for missing people."

Soon Tom and Liz were at the luggage carousel, waiting for their suitcases. Mrs. Austen was at the Tilden desk renting a car, Liz was watching some emotional reunions taking place, and Tom's eyes were on three men. They'd come off the flight together and were dressed identically in camouflage gear like something out of a violent war video. Their heads were close-shaved and their faces were grim.

Tom glanced at Liz. "What do you make of them?"

"Organized trouble."

"Their stuff's arriving on the carousel. Those bundles look like tents."

"Check out the expensive duffel bags."

"Maybe they're hunters."

"Yeah, but what are they hunting?"

Liz helped Tom take their luggage off the carousel, then said, "I'll go tell Mom everything's accounted for."

"Okay, and I'll wait here with our stuff. Listen, try again to convince Mom to rent a BMW. Tilden has a special on German cars this month."

"You dreamer," Liz said. "But I'll give it a try."

Tom watched the three heavies exit the building. A fourth man was waiting outside with a rental van; strapped to the roof was a powerful outboard engine and a big rubber raft that looked like a Zodiac. The men heaved their equipment into the van and drove off, leaving a trail of white exhaust in the chill November air.

Tom looked down at the suitcases, counting them again, but was startled by the approach of two people. One was the man who'd been sitting beside him on the jet, and the other was a younger woman who was also dressed in a leather jacket, jeans and cowboy boots. She had a beautiful face with high cheekbones and brown eyes; in her left ear were three sapphire studs.

"Hey, kid," the man said. "About that letter you were talking about — I want to know where it was mailed from."

The woman watched Tom closely. When he didn't speak, she grabbed his jacket in both hands. "Answer him!"

The man gestured at her. "Take it easy! You're attracting attention."

Letting Tom go, she looked around. People were staring, including Mrs. Austen and Liz as they approached from the rental counter. The man motioned the woman toward the exit, and, as they walked away, he stared at Tom.

2

Driving into the city in the rental Chev, Tom and Liz discovered 590-VOCM on the radio until Mrs. Austen asked for something quieter. They tuned in an FM country station just as the DJ was introducing a Rodney Crowell song that he'd written after his father's death.

Nobody spoke as they listened to the singer's faith in being reunited with his father some day. Then Liz squeezed her mother's hand. "We're sorry."

Tom nodded. "We love you, Mom."

Brushing away a tear, she managed a smile. "At least I've got nothing to regret. All my life I showed her my love, just like you kids have always done."

The sun was low in the sky, turning Tom's hair even

redder as he gazed at the old Victorian houses they were passing. "Excellent locations for murders or ghosts! I can't believe I'm actually in North America's oldest city. There must be a million stories to hear."

Mrs. Austen nodded. "Your relatives know a lot. I hope you've got a full supply of notebooks."

Liz smiled. "I saw him packing them. Right beside all the film for his new camera."

Mrs. Austen looked at Tom in the mirror. "I'm glad you're finally getting a chance to meet your cousins, especially with the way Duncan keeps sending you those admiring letters. Maybe one day they'll have a chance to visit Winnipeg."

On a hillside above the harbour, Mrs. Austen stopped at an old-fashioned house that rose three stories above the sidewalk. "This is the Prescott Inn, the bed-and-breakfast where we'll be staying. I've rented us each a room. The prices are very reasonable in November."

Inside, they met a friendly young woman with blond hair. "Welcome to the Inn," she said. "I'm Sherry, and I've been expecting you. On the phone you told me about your Mom," she said to Mrs. Austen as they climbed the stairs. "I'm sorry."

"Thanks, Sherry. I appreciate your concern."

"There's two bedrooms on each floor. Tom and Liz have rooms at the top of the stairs, since they've got the youngest legs." She smiled at them. "Do you like the paintings on the walls? Artists leave us their work, hoping guests may buy them."

"This snowy owl is incredible," Liz said. "Look at the fierce yellow eyes. I wouldn't want to be its prey." Her room had a small fireplace, walls of royal blue, and lace curtains that billowed at the open window. Outside was a large yard; down the hill, the harbour and cliffs were shadowed as evening approached. "The sun will be setting soon. Let's go look around."

"I'll stay and unpack," Mrs. Austen said. "Then I'm going to the hospital to visit Nanny. Maybe you could find something to eat, in case I'm home late."

"There's a take-out fish and chips place," Sherry said. "Just around the corner."

Mrs. Austen gave Tom and Liz some money. "Bring your meal home to eat, okay? I'll phone if I'm going to be late."

Liz nodded. "Give our love to Nanny." She stumbled on the words, and almost started crying. "Tell her we'll be there tomorrow."

*   *   *

Outside in the cold air they wandered past the ancient seaport's houses of stone and wood. A few yellow leaves hung from the bare branches of trees as the city awaited winter, with shovels and brooms positioned by front doors and trees wrapped against the coming cold.

As Tom took a picture of the beautiful old houses, Liz said hello to a passing cat. "What a beauty," she said. "I think the weather's going to change. See how restless she is?"

"That's just a superstition."

"Maybe so, but I'll stick to my forecast."

At a store called Kelly's Korner, they met some kids who asked if they were from up-along. "What's that mean?" Liz asked.

"From the mainland," a boy replied. He watched Tom write the expression in his notebook. "Been screeched in yet?" When Tom shook his head, the boy grinned. "That'll be some entertainment."

As they continued on their walk, Tom and Liz tried to figure out what the boy had meant. In the distance, at the end of the harbour, sunset colours glinted from the windows of a subdivision which rose toward a cliff above. The harbour waters had turned a steely blue, the surface rippled with waves. Lights shone from the highrise business towers near the docks, and in the shops and houses on the hills of the city.

"What a great shot," Tom said, taking a picture. His face tingled in the cold air.

Liz nodded. "Take one of that classic house over there with the balconies on top of each bay window. Wouldn't you like to catch some rays on one of these decks in the summer?"

"I'd like to be on a balcony right now, holding a good pair of binoculars. The view of the harbour is perfect, and most ports are crawling with crime. People could be inside those container vessels trying to get into the country, or maybe spies are hiding in submarines offshore. Can't you just picture someone being smuggled into this port at midnight, then taking cover in one of these old stone houses?"

"Who do you think those cowboys are? Why'd they want to know where Duncan's letter was mailed?"

"I don't know," Tom replied, "but they're definitely interested in the Ice Diamond, whatever that means. Do you suppose it's some kind of famous jewel?"

"Maybe. In school we've been studying the Crown Jewels of Britain — they're kept under guard in the Tower of London. One of them is a diamond called the Mountain of Light, and on the video it looked the size of an egg."

"Wow! Imagine what it's worth."

Liz nodded. "I have a feeling those cowboys came to Newfoundland to find the Ice Diamond. Maybe they want to know where Duncan lives so they can go there and watch for the yacht to signal."

"Let's do some research while we're in St. John's. If the Ice Diamond's a famous jewel, maybe we can find something about it at the library."

"Good idea," Liz said, "and we could ask at some jewellery stores." She looked at her watch. "Hey! It's getting late, and we promised to phone Dad this evening. We'd better head back."

"Let's not forget the fish and chips." Tom rubbed his stomach with a gloved hand. "I'm getting worse than Dietmar Oban for the munchies."

"It's this sea air."

Liz looked up at the silhouette of a jet circling in the pale sky above the harbour. She sniffed the air, certain the weather was about to change.

*   *   *

An hour later, a wind slammed through the harbour entrance and raced up the hill, shaking the Prescott Inn. Liz was sitting on her bed eating the last of her fish and chips and reading *The Hound of the Baskervilles*.

"Is that the wind?" she said to herself, as the Inn began to sway. "Or an earthquake?" The chimney howled, and the floor moved before Liz's eyes. But she kept her emotions under control — until a fist hammered against the door.

"*Ey-yah!*" Rolling off the bed she dropped into an oriental defence stance. "Who's there?"

"Me! Your brother, Tom. Who else would it be?"

Liz turned to the window and pretended to look out. "Enter," she called in a dignified voice.

Tom rushed in, gesturing toward the staircase. "Someone's ringing the doorbell downstairs, over and over. We'd better see if something's wrong. Sherry's out for the evening, and Mom's not home yet."

"Okay, let's check," Liz said. "I thought I heard something ringing, but I figured the storm caused it."

"The wind's dying down," Tom said, as they cautiously descended the stairs, listening to the doorbell ring. Light from a glass chandelier shone in the entrance hallway, illuminating the tall door with its oval window. Through it they could see a woman in a police cap, gesturing excitedly. "Help," she cried, her voice muffled by the door. "There's been a bad accident!"

Tom looked at his sister. "It was the wind! Someone's been blasted right off the road."

Hurrying to the door, they unlocked it and stepped onto the sidewalk. But there was no sign of an accident. The woman stood in the shadows, but they saw now that she wore a fake police cap. Nearby, a black Jeep was parked at the curb with its motor running. The word RENEGADE was written on the Jeep in big silver letters. It had no passenger doors.

Stepping out of the Jeep was the cowboy from the plane. "I've wasted enough time on you," he said, walking toward them. "I want an answer, and I want it now. Tell me about that letter."

"Let's move it," Liz shouted, racing across the street with Tom. They ran swiftly toward the dark shadows of some trees, but were stopped by a spiked iron fence. The wind storm was over, leaving the night silent except for traffic on nearby streets.

"Those Renegades!" Tom cried, pointing at the couple in the Jeep. "They're coming after us!"

The Jeep burned rubber as it left the Prescott Inn and roared up the street. The man and woman leaned out the open doors searching for Tom and Liz, but went past without seeing them stretched low on the ground.

"How'd they know where to find us?" Tom whispered.

"Maybe they followed us into town from the airport, then watched the Inn until we were alone. Sherry just went home, remember? They're sure desperate to know where Duncan lives. The signal from the yacht is really important to them."

"Got your key for the Inn?" Tom asked. "I didn't bring mine."

Liz shook her head. "I guess we're locked out until Mom gets home."

"Let's head downtown, just in case those Renegades keep searching. We may need help."

The street descended steeply to the harbour. Houses stood like oversized kids' blocks, each a bit lower than its neighbour. A few people were around, but the city's small size meant the streets were mostly quiet all the way to the harbour. Above the cliffs a full moon filled the velvet night.

"Hey," Tom said, "here's a back alley. There's docks at the end — I can see a trawler. Let's go check it out."

"It's pretty dark down there."

"Maybe . . . ."

Tom was interrupted by the roar of a Jeep rounding a corner onto Water Street. Halogen headlights glared in their eyes, and a voice yelled *"I see those kids!"*

They darted into the alley and ran swiftly toward the dock; Tom looked at the white trawler with the flag of Japan at its stern, then he motioned Liz toward the gangplank. "No one's on deck. Maybe they've all got shore leave."

"We've got to hide somewhere!" Stepping onto the steel deck, Liz wrinkled her nose. "Fish." As headlights flashed against the vessel's funnel she ducked behind a lifeboat with Tom. "Let's get inside this thing. We can hide under the canvas cover."

Quickly they struggled into the lifeboat. As they pulled

the cover back into place they heard the Jeep stop, then cautious footsteps on the gangplank.

"You're wrong," the man's voice said. "Those kids aren't on this boat."

"It's the only possible hiding place."

"They're slippery like eels, those two. They could be anywhere."

The heels of cowboy boots clanged away along the steel deck. Tom and Liz breathed quietly, not daring to move. Then suddenly the canvas was ripped back, and they saw the face of the cowboy.

"Got you," he said, smiling.

3

The woman returned to the lifeboat, her boots noisy on the deck. "Thought you could fool us? Well, I'm here to . . . ."

Liz opened her mouth and yelled, *"Tasukete!"* The couple stared at her in shock as she repeated the cry: *"Tasukete!"* A light switched on behind a nearby porthole, then a door opened and a voice called out in Japanese.

"Tasukete," Liz shouted. *"Tasukete!"*

Lights were springing on all over the trawler. The man swore, gave Tom and Liz a dirty look, then took off running with his partner. As the Jeep tore away into the night, a ship's officer ran to the lifeboat.

He unleashed a flood of Japanese at Liz but she shook

her head, gesturing sorry. "I don't speak your language."

"But," he said, "you cried for help in Japanese."

Liz grinned. "My friend Makiko taught me a few words. But I never thought I'd use them!"

* * *

The next morning they were in Nanny's hospital room. Her skin was terribly pale, but her blue eyes were bright. "Of course the captain of that trawler called the police?" she asked. "What did they do?"

"Took all the information and drove us home. They don't know what Ice Diamond means so they'll keep it a secret while they investigate. Unfortunately we didn't get the Renagades' licence number — it was smeared with mud."

"Could they be hired criminals, working for some local person who wants to find the Ice Diamond?"

"Sure, that's possible," Tom said.

"We have to tell our story again today," Liz told her grandmother. "The manager of the port wants us to answer some questions."

Nanny reached out to them with shaking, frail hands. "I'm proud of you both. Your letters over the years gave me so much pleasure, and I loved every visit to Winnipeg."

Tom squeezed back his tears. "Us too."

"I spoke to your father this morning." Nanny paused, gathering strength. "He called from Arizona, apologizing again for not being here. I told him that it's much more important to help find those missing people."

Mrs. Austen shook her head. "I'm glad Ted can help other police departments, but I wouldn't mind seeing more of him."

Nanny smiled at Tom and Liz. "I'd like a private chat

with your mother. How about getting something to eat at the hospital cafeteria, then come back and join us."

"Sure, Nanny."

Liz and Tom gently hugged their grandmother, then went into the corridor. A man with a hunched back was advancing on them with glittering eyes. Liz smiled at him. "Excuse me sir, I just wanted to say thank you."

He stopped beside his laundry cart. "What for?"

"Nanny says you talk to her when the nurses are busy, even during your lunch break. You've listened to all her stories about Petty Harbour — she loved that."

"Your grandmother's a spellbinder." The man shook hands with them. "I'm sorry she's dying."

"Thanks," they both said quietly.

*   *   *

After talking again to Nanny, they left the hospital. Sniffling sadly, they burrowed down in their coats in the clear, cold air. "I bet sea captains used to live on this street," Liz said as they walked toward the harbour. "That's what these houses look like."

"Know why they're painted all these colours? The sea air eats away the paint. When it's redone, the owners pick something else really bright. It cheers up the foggy days."

"Who told you that?"

"It's in that Newfoundland tourist guide I was reading on the plane. Know what else I found out? Government House was built with a moat around it."

"How come? There weren't knights over here."

"To keep out lizards and snakes." Tom smiled. "But the architect made a mistake — there aren't any reptiles in Newfoundland."

As they walked down the hill, Tom took several pictures of beautiful old houses. Downtown, they followed crowded streets of highrise glass towers, stores and seafood restaurants to the Port Manager's building. It was brick, standing alone by the harbour. They went upstairs to an office where a man worked at a desk. "I'm Dave Foster," he said, shaking hands. He had white hair and a handsome face, and was dressed in a suit that looked expensive.

"Are we in major trouble?" Tom asked.

"That's for my boss to decide. Come meet her." He led them into an adjoining office. It was very large, with art on the walls, a desk and office furniture, and, in one corner, there were sofas and a coffee table.

Outside the windows they saw the harbour's blue waters and many docks, with seagulls and stormy clouds above. Tom didn't notice the spectacular view. Instead, his eyes were fixed on the woman who sat behind the desk. Looking like a model in a fashion magazine, she wore an elegant white suit and make-up that complimented her large azure eyes. Her glasses had bright red frames, and her long dark hair was beautiful.

"I'm Kathy Munro, the Port Manager," she said, standing up. She was tall and her eyes were very blue. "You must be Tom and Liz Austen. It's nice of you to pay me a visit."

"About last night, we . . . ."

"Don't worry about it, you're not in trouble. I just want a few details for my report — I've already spoken to the captain of the trawler. Any more news about those cowboy types?"

"Not a word," Tom replied.

"Why do they want to know about an Ice Diamond? Any theories?"

"My cousin wrote me about spotting a signal from sea," Tom replied. "It probably contained the words Ice

Diamond. On the plane I was discussing his letter with my sister when that guy nosed in."

"Why do you suppose they're so desperate for information?"

Tom shook his head. "We don't know anything, except for the Ice Diamond connection. Those Renegades are trying to find out where my cousin posted his letter. I guess so they can watch for that signal themselves."

"Or maybe search around there for the Ice Diamond," Kathy suggested. "Where does your cousin live, anyway?"

"Petty Harbour."

"A beautiful place, I understand," she said, making a note. "I've been hoping to see Petty Harbour in person, but my work keeps me chained to this desk. I moved to Newfoundland only a few months ago."

"What's your job?" Liz asked.

"I'm responsible for the ships, cargoes and crews using this port. It's demanding, but I love the sea." She looked out the window. "See the harbour mouth, where the cliffs almost meet? Think about the stories that have sailed through there over the centuries."

"What's that stone place, up on the cliff? It looks like a castle."

"That's Cabot Tower. It was built to honour 400 years of Newfoundland history."

"I read about U-boats firing torpedoes at this harbour during the last war," Tom said. "Did they destroy much?"

"They missed every time," Kathy replied. "I guess that harbour opening was a difficult shot. It's called the Narrows." She motioned at a notebook on her desk. "I've been writing down the local expressions. Understanding Newfoundland culture will help me get to the top. I'm determined to be a success."

"Is this port crawling with crime?" Tom asked.

"Nothing out of the ordinary, except perhaps for the spies who've entered Canada through here."

"I knew it!" Tom grinned at his sister. "One to me."

"Yup." Liz turned to Kathy. "May I ask a personal question?"

"Sure."

"Have you been engaged long? Your ring is really shiny."

"Exactly fourteen days. You're very observant!"

Liz grinned. "I've used that trick before."

Kathy led them to a window overlooking some docks. "See that vessel? It's a perfect replica of an ancient sealing schooner. A man named Richard Livingstone just had it built. During the old days Richard's family made a fortune sending schooners out to the ice for seals — people all over the world wore sealskin coats and hats. The Livingstones had a huge office on Water Street, but protests eventually stopped the sealing. These days Richard runs the family company, Livingtone Sea Profits, from smaller premises. I met him in an elevator soon after moving here — it was very romantic! He's a charming man, and definitely easy on the eyes. Anyway, he's the man I'm supposed to marry."

"Congratulations," Liz said. "That's great."

"Thanks," Kathy said with a quick grin.

Tom studied her face. "Why'd you say *supposed* to marry?"

Kathy frowned. "Richard lives in a family mansion that's really old, with stone walls and stained-glass windows and probably some ghosts for all I know. Anyway, there isn't much left of the family fortune. There's no servants in his mansion now, so Richard does it all. He insists on completely refurnishing the place *before* we get married. He also wants a new car for our honeymoon, and . . . ." Her voice trailed off. Going to the window, she looked at the distant schooner. "Sometimes I worry about Richard's business smarts. He's sunk the last of the family money, and some hefty bank loans, into that boat. He expects to make money with it, but sometimes I wonder. If it fails, he'll lose everything."

"What's his plan?" Tom asked.

"In the summer he'll take tourists on journeys to see the coast of Labrador and meet some of the locals. That part makes sense, and it'll work. But the schooner also has to generate money in the winter to pay off the bank loans. Richard's got a plan in mind, but . . . ." She ran a hand through her long black hair. "Frankly, I don't think it'll work."

"What's involved? More sea cruises?"

"Sort of, I guess. He wants to take adventurous people out to the ice. They'll experience how the sealers used to live, and even explore the floes to see the seals and their pups. Richard says they're an amazing sight."

"It sounds like a neat experience," Liz said.

"Sure, but Richard's going to charge a small fortune. Who'll pay the money? That's what worries me."

The door opened, and Dave Foster entered with a large tray. On it was a silver coffee urn, a porcelain cup and saucer, cookies and delicate sandwiches, and glasses of apple juice.

"Feel like a snack?" he asked, putting the tray on the coffee table. As the others sat down on the comfortable sofas, he poured coffee for Kathy.

"It's delicious today," the man said to her. "I bought it especially for you in a little shop I found downtown. You'll love it." He smiled at her. "Any extras I can do for you, Kathy? Any errands that need running?"

"Thanks Dave, but no."

As he left the room and closed the door, Kathy sipped her coffee. "Dave's a handsome man, and very nice, but he's my secretary. I can't marry him."

"Is that what he wants?" Liz asked.

"He hasn't said yet, but I think so." She passed them sandwiches. "Dave makes these for me every day. It's not in his job description, but he insists."

"I bet your wedding to Richard will be a major social event," Liz said. "After all, if he's from an old sealing family and lives in a mansion, lots of people will want to attend."

Kathy nodded. "That's another problem, the cost of the wedding. The way Richard is planning it, there'll be hundreds of guests. But he says he can afford it. There's something mysterious happening in his life right now. I know it involves big money, but he won't say a word — except that this secret project will pay for everything we'll need — forever."

"I'd like to know more about that project," Tom said.

"I've got an idea," Kathy said. "Would you like to meet Richard and visit the schooner? I love the sea, so perhaps we could go somewhere. Hey, I know! Richard's sailing to Petty Harbour soon. Maybe we could give you a ride down there."

"Sounds great," Tom said.

"It'll be cold this time of year, but you're from Winnipeg. I've heard about the corner of Portage and Main — you won't even notice this wind!"

For a moment Kathy looked at the schooner, then she turned to Tom and Liz. "Lately I've been worried. I'm convinced there's a threat to Richard. Don't ask me why, but I can sense danger."

*   *   *

Kathy had no proof, but Liz still shivered. "What does Richard think about your fears?"

"He laughs them off, usually. But he's been very quiet recently. Maybe meeting you two will cheer him up." She motioned at the coffee table. "Let's eat Dave's snack."

Tom looked at a framed photograph on the wall. "Where's that? Somewhere in Europe?"

Kathy nodded. "That's the German town where my car was manufactured. It's an enchanting place, and I keep hoping to return. I went over there to collect the car, then I toured Europe. What a wonderful experience."

"That's what I'm doing when I'm older," Liz said. She picked up a copy of *Maclean's* from the glass table. "Have they got anything about that Prince?"

"You bet," Kathy said. "Turn to page 23. Isn't it a fascinating story?" Liz opened the magazine to a picture of a handsome boy, about 18, with dark eyes and thick black hair. "That's a computer-assisted photograph," Kathy explained. "The only known picture of the Prince shows him at age three, so a computer decided what he looks like today."

"Who's this prince?" Tom asked.

"Fifteen years ago there was a revolution in his country," Kathy said. "The Prince, aged three, was smuggled out when revolutionaries seized the throne. He's been raised in secret hideouts ever since."

"When he turns 18," Liz added, "the crown is supposed to be his. He'll probably come out of hiding, and try to get his country back."

"Unless he's stopped," Kathy added. "The people who now control the country are searching for the Prince's hiding place. If they can kill him, they won't lose their grip on power."

Liz studied the magazine. "I wonder how the computer did this picture. It's so realistic."

Kathy stood up and looked out the window. "Would

you care to see the exact place where Terry Fox and Steve Fonyo started their runs across Canada?"

"For sure!"

"It's just outside this building."

As they passed through the outer office Dave Foster looked up from his computer. "Are you leaving?"

"We're just going outside, Dave, to see a bit of history." She reached for a suede coat hanging in the closet, but Dave Foster jumped up and grabbed it first. "Let me help," he said, holding the coat for Kathy.

Outside the building Tom got his camera ready as they approached the shore. Water lapped around jagged chunks of rock under his feet, and machinery roared at a nearby dock where a ship was being loaded.

"I don't see a monument," he said.

"The ceremonial start to each run was at City Hall, but they both dipped their artifical legs in the Atlantic at this exact spot."

Tom took some time to set up a picture, then bent down to touch the water. "I'm really glad to visit here — every September we do the Terry Fox run."

"Would you care to see the easternmost place in all of North America? We could drive there."

"Sure!" Tom said. "That would be great."

"I planned some time off this afternoon to work on my new house. It's an old place, very beautiful, but it's costing a fortune to get ready — way more than I expected. I wouldn't mind an excuse to avoid it today."

"Cape Spear sounds like a neat place," Liz said.

"Yes," Kathy replied. "But at times it's scary."

*   *   *

Before the trip, Tom obeyed his mother's stern instructions and got a haircut. The barbershop on Duckworth

Street had comfortable leather chairs, and barbers who spoke with lilting accents. "That's the Irish in us," one man explained. "Our ancestors sailed across the Atlantic generations ago. They came to make a new life, along with people from other countries like England."

A second man broke into a soft-shoe dance, then returned to solemnly clipping hair. "We've still got their love of music and a good party."

"I'm a Newfoundlander, too," Tom said. "My Mom was born in Petty Harbour. We'll be there soon, and I'll see my cousin Duncan. He's like me, kind of interested in mysteries. Duncan spotted a signal from sea, and I'm anxious to know more."

"What was the signal?" a barber asked. He was applying heated towels to the face of a man who leaned far back in a chair.

"I'm not sure, but it included the words Ice Diamond."

Suddenly the towels were knocked away as the man sat up. His skin had been weathered by strong sun and winds, and his hair was black, with streaks of grey. For long moments he stared at Tom with black eyes as fierce as a hawk's, then finally leaned back and motioned for the barber to apply more towels.

Tom gulped. "I forgot, it's a secret." His barber also looked upset, and continued the haircut in silence. Later, as Tom was paying, the man said, "Visited Cape Spear yet? It's quite the place."

"We're going there today. See those people waiting for me in the car? That woman's taking us. She says it's the most easterly place in North America."

Leaving the barber shop, Tom took a deep breath of sea air. Then he studied the car. "Nice unit," he said, getting in. "Do you have stereo?"

"It's not my car," Kathy replied. "I borrowed it from my secretary — see if you can figure out his music system. We'll make a pit stop at Tim Horton's before leaving town."

"Kathy, I blundered." Tom's face glowed red. "In the barbershop I talked about the Ice Diamond. I forgot it's a police secret."

"Don't worry about it, Tom. We all make mistakes."

At the doughnut shop they bought apple crullers and other goodies, then sat at a small table. Around them people were reading newspapers, laughing together, discussing politics. Cars rushed past outside, heading for a big mall.

Liz looked at Kathy. "I love the red frames on your glasses, they're so classy."

"Thanks, Liz."

"I may give my contacts a rest, and go back to glasses. I could get some fancy ones like yours. Were they expensive?"

"Kind of."

"I was afraid of that." Pouting, Liz looked out at the passing traffic. "I guess I'll stay with my contacts."

Kathy smiled. "Have you heard the latest scoop on the Prince? Apparently a faithful servant is involved, the same guy who smuggled the Prince out of his country at age three, and he's raised him in hiding ever since. Some reporter just broke the story — she tracked the Prince and his servant to New Zealand."

"Are they still hiding in New Zealand?" Tom asked.

"Nobody knows, but by the time she broke the story the Prince had moved on from that hideout. He's gone secretly from country to country over the years, and he's still on the run."

"But in a few days he turns 18," Liz said, "and can come out of hiding to claim his throne. Won't it be exciting? That computer photo made him look so handsome!"

Tom looked at Kathy. "Why'd you call Cape Spear a

scary place?"

"In winter it's so bleak, with the wind howling off those cold, grey seas. During the last war, huge guns guarded the harbour entrance from the cape. You can still see them. What a lonely posting for the soldiers."

Leaving St. John's they passed many homes with the unique Newfoundland flag fluttering from poles. Outside the city, thick forest stretched toward Cape Spear, and to the north they could see the Narrows and the shadowed cliffs battered by leaping waves.

"Okay to stop for a picture?" Tom asked. As the car pulled over he focussed on the distant cliff where the Cabot Tower guarded the harbour. "Newfoundland's so big, it's hard to believe it's an island."

Kathy looked at the vast, empty sea. "My Grandfather served out there during the last war. He was in a ship escorting freighters with supplies for the war in Europe. Gramps used to describe the stormy seas, and how he'd wonder where the pack of enemy submarines was lying in wait. Those people in the armed forces were so brave."

Soon they were approaching the Cape. Out at sea, thick fog was advancing ashore. They climbed to the top of the barren rock where Tom posed the others beside the lighthouse. "Just in time," he said. "The fog's about to hide everything."

As wet, grey cloud swirled around, the powerful beam of the lighthouse swept the sky and a foghorn groaned. "It's getting dark," Kathy said. "I'm going back to the car."

Tom was disappointed. "May I see those big guns from the war?"

"Sure! Meet me at the car."

"I'll go with my brother," Liz said.

"Okay."

There'd been other people at the Cape earlier, but it

was deserted as Tom and Liz followed a path down a steep slope. To one side was the enormous glacial rock, to the other was fog, hiding the long drop. From below in the mist came the thudding of waves against the cape.

"Kathy's right," Liz said. "This is a lonely place."

They entered a concrete tunnel and followed it to other tunnels. Water stained the walls, and dripped into puddles. "There's one of those big guns," Tom said, pointing at a place where the tunnels emerged, high above the sea. "That barrel easily looks 10 metres long!" Near the gun, built into the rock, were concrete bunkers connected by the tunnels. "Maybe the soldiers lived here. There's a sign with some information — let's read it."

As Tom stood beside the sign, making notes, Liz seemed very quiet. Finally he glanced her way and gasped — she was gone.

"Liz?"

Tom looked at the fog and the concrete bunkers. Their windows were stained by rust from metal frames, and had no glass. He tiptoed into a tunnel, trying to see through the fog. "Liz?" His voice echoed with a hollow sound. "Where are you?"

Around a dark corner Tom continued slowly forward, then his face was touched by something cold. With a yell he swung around, and saw his grinning sister holding a chunk of wild grass.

Tom took a deep breath. "Let's get out of here."

Liz nodded. "Good idea."

Outside the tunnels they followed a path until the parking lot appeared ahead. "There's Kathy, waiting by the path," Liz said. "I guess we're late." She held up an apologetic hand. "Sorry, Kathy. Tom took forever making notes."

Before he could protest, the headlights of a car came out of the darkness. Entering the parking lot, it stopped when the beams caught them. Then a door slammed. As fog danced past the headlights, a man appeared.

"Hey," Liz said. "Isn't he the guy from the barber shop, the one who went strange when you mentioned the Ice Diamond? He fits your description exactly."

Tom nodded. "In my notes I call him the Hawk."

"Perfect name."

"Let's get in the car," Kathy said.

As they walked to it, the man remained motionless, watching them. Then he raised a hand and pointed at Tom.

"Leave this island," he said. *"Immediately."*

4

The next morning, Liz stood at her window. Down at the harbour, seagulls soared on a wind that swept in from the stormy Atlantic. In the yard below, a calico cat prowled through autumn leaves, then leapt to the porch of a bright red house. At the yellow house next door, smoke from a chimney tumbled away on the wind.

"What a day for adventure," Liz said to her brother, entering the big kitchen on the ground floor of the bed-and-breakfast. "I'm so hungry! Maybe Richard Livingstone will take us for a sail on his schooner today. We could go after seeing Nanny."

"Mom just phoned from the hospital," Tom said. "Nanny's really weak, we can't visit her."

Liz looked at the bowl of eggs on the tile counter, the glass jar filled with granola, and the sugary loaf of home-made bread. "Maybe I'll eat something later."

"I'm not hungry, either."

"Let's walk down to the harbour and see Richard's schooner."

"Okay, but how about some investigating first?" Tom studied his map of St. John's. "It's not far to the public library. Let's try there for information on the Ice Diamond."

*   *   *

At the library the Austens leaned over many dusty books, using the computer to check some complicated references — but the search led nowhere. Outside, they walked together to Water Street. The wind off the Atlantic was cold, blowing past the highrise office towers and making shoppers bend low as they hurried along the streets.

"There's a jewellery store," Tom said, pointing at a wooden sign creaking in the wind above a doorway. "Maybe they'd know something."

In the store, a young man was behind the counter. His spectacles were small circles reflecting the light, he was going bald, and his clothes were from an earlier decade. He listened to Tom and Liz, then chuckled.

"No such jewel exists. I know every name, famous and infamous. Ice Diamond means nothing to me." Looking out the window, he stroked his moustache. "Makes me think, though. On clear winter days here the sun sparkles off the ice. Always reminds me of diamonds." He glanced at a Grandfather Clock ticking solemnly in the corner. "Run along you two. I've got work to do."

Back outside on Water Street, Tom made some notes.

"What did you think of the jeweller? Was he telling the truth?"

"Maybe," Liz replied, "but let's do some more checking. The Ice Diamond is definitely real, or those Renegades wouldn't be after us. If it's not a jewel, what is it?"

*   *   *

At the harbour, waves chased each other across the dark water. Tom and Liz quickly spotted the schooner beside a dock. The wooden boat was very unusual, with its old-fashioned deck and schooner-rigged sails.

It was being studied by a couple who had white hair and friendly faces. "This is an excellent replica," the woman said. She smiled. "I'm Eve Mulcahy, and this is my husband Pat. We live by the sea, but we've never seen anything like this schooner."

Her husband pointed to the stern. "See how the rudder's mounted outside? That's to keep it free of ice. Sealers faced tough conditions, especially on the early schooners. Eventually the companies used engines, and boats with metal hulls, but it was still rough for the men."

Mrs. Mulcahy nodded. "There's been some real tragedies. After the terrible sealing disaster of 1914, thousands lined these docks to watch ships returning home with the frozen bodies of their men. They were stacked on deck like cordwood."

"I just bought a book about that disaster," Tom said. "It's called *Death on the Ice*. Have you read it?"

"Oh my, yes."

"Why'd those men freeze?" Liz asked.

"They were out on the ice, far from their boat," Tom replied. "A blizzard trapped them."

"But why were they on the ice? Didn't the captain

know a storm was coming?"

"Certainly," Mrs. Mulcahy said, "but he took a chance. He really needed seal pelts, so the men were ordered onto the ice. They were far from the boat when the blizzard struck. They didn't have a chance."

"Did the captain get into trouble with his company?"

"Not a chance, my dear. Local people called the sealing companies the pirates of Water Street, because they were so greedy for money. They didn't care what happened to the men."

"Of course," her husband said, "that was long ago. Now young Livingstone has built this schooner. It's quite a project! I admire him."

Mrs. Mulcahy smiled at him. "We don't always agree, darling. Now let's go — it's time to shop."

The couple said goodbye, leaving Tom and Liz to study the schooner. The wood was new, brass and paint gleamed, ropes and canvas were still shiny. Near the stern was a large wheelhouse with outside power controls for the engine. On top of the wheelhouse was a big plexiglass bubble; inside it could be seen two leather bucket seats facing a wheel and power controls. A man sat in one chair, studying the harbour with binoculars. Putting them down, he noticed Tom and Liz and smiled a welcome.

Moments later he appeared on deck. He was about 45 years old. "Hi, I'm Richard Livingstone. I've been watching for you." He was wearing deck boots and foul weather gear, and looked like a runner. His thick brown hair was turning silver, and his green eyes were friendly. "Welcome aboard the *Quest*."

"It's beautiful," Tom said.

"Kathy suggested I take you for a trip. We'll arrange one for sure." Richard pointed out the vessel's schooner rigging, and explained the arrangement of sails, then gave a mast a proud slap. "The *Quest* cost me a lot, but I don't mind. I'm a Livingstone. My family's ships have sailed from this harbour for generations, and Grandfather alone made a fortune from the sealing trade. I'll be taking people out to see the seal pups that made the Livingstone name famous."

"Sounds like a great idea," Liz said, smiling at Richard.

"The pups are protected now, aren't they?" Tom asked.

"Actually, my guests will be shooting them." When Tom stared at him in horror, Richard grinned. "But only with video cameras!"

"You got me." Tom looked at two rubber boats with big outboard motors powering across the harbour. "Those Zodiacs are really moving!"

"That looks like a Coast Guard exercise." Richard studied the Zodiacs with his binoculars, then trained them on a hill rising above St. John's. "In six months, work starts on Livingstone Park. I'm donating it to the city."

"That's wonderful," Liz said. "There should be parks everywhere."

Richard's face glowed. "Thanks!"

"What gave you the idea of making a park?"

"I want to honour my family name, and especially my grandfather. He took a lot of abuse during the sealing protests. It was rough — so this park is important!"

"Why wait six months to start?" Tom asked.

"There's some dumpy old houses and apartment buildings that need to be knocked down. The people living there have six months to be out."

"Where will they go?"

Richard beamed. "I've promised them beautiful accomodations in Livingstone Villas. It's a revolutionary new vision in housing. It'll have everything, even indoor pools. I tell you, the people of this province love my plans. They can't wait for Livingstone Park to be built."

"Mom wants us to touch the statue of Peter Pan in Bowring Park," Liz said. "She says that's a local tradition."

Richard frowned. "The Bowrings were rivals of my grandfather." He showed them the wheel and controls attached to the outside of the wheelhouse. Then he opened a door to narrow wooden steps that led down inside the cabin.

"Watch your heads," Richard warned. "I had this schooner built from original plans, and people were smaller in those days."

Yellow oil lamps hung from wooden beams, lighting the shadowed cabin. Above, the white sky was seen through the plexiglass bubble. It sheltered the inside controls and twin bucket seats on their raised platform.

"See that brass cage?" Richard said. "When I go to sea, I'll be taking Henry with me. He's a parrot."

"Neat!" Tom exclaimed.

Richard picked up a kettle from an old-fashioned stove. "I'm learning to prepare tea," he explained. "The same brew as the captains and men once drank. The tourists will love the authenticity."

"The sealers slept on these wooden bunks?" Liz sat on the rough lumber. "Where are the mattresses?"

"None in those days. Too expensive, I guess."

"Your tourists are willing to sleep on bare wood?"

Richard smiled. "Some people may, just for the experience, but I've got small mattresses stowed away for the others. I do have some modern things, you know, like the plexiglass dome and those inside controls. I don't like getting soaked on deck during storms."

Tom looked around. Oilskins hung from pegs, and there were seaboots, but nothing of comfort. "People are actually going to pay money for this?"

"Sure thing, Tom. Adventure holidays are totally in with bored executives."

Tom studied some barrels stacked in a corner, then looked at displays of food from the early days of sealing. "You've worked hard."

Richard looked at him. His eyes were serious. "That's where success comes from, Tom, hard work and brains. I studied the market before I built this schooner, and I've filled it with genuine artifacts." He picked up the kettle. "This was actually used by sealers on a wooden-waller. People want to see the real thing!"

"What's a wooden-waller?" Liz asked.

"A sealing schooner with a wooden hull, just like the *Quest*. Later the companies converted to metal hulls." Richard lifted an oilskin from a wooden peg on the wall. "See the name Hunter inside here? That's who actually owned this oilskin."

"He was a small man," Tom said.

"Actually, Hunter was about the same age as you."

"Kids my age went sealing?"

"Sure, and they were glad of the work. No jobs serving hamburgers in those days!"

"Where'd you find the oilskin?" Liz asked.

"Way up the coast, in a tiny outport. It was a family heirloom, passed from generation to generation. They wanted too much money, but I talked them down." Richard grinned. "Actually, bargaining with that family wasn't much of a challenge. There hadn't been work for some time, so they were desperate for cash. I got a nice deal."

Up at the bucket seats, they watched Richard demonstrate the controls. Then he grabbed a power megaphone, and led them out on deck. The pale November sky seemed brilliant after the gloomy cabin. They tried bouncing their voices off the cliffs across the harbour, then Richard switched off the megaphone and sighed happily.

"Life's so good! I've got the *Quest,* and I'll soon be married again. My first wife demanded too much so I divorced her, but Kathy's different — she's the woman of my dreams." He winked at Tom. "Isn't she something wonderful?"

"She's really beautiful!"

Richard nodded. "You bet. Everywhere I take Kathy, heads turn. Men stare, and I know what they're thinking. They all want to be Richard Livingstone."

"Sounds wonderful," Liz said. "What's in it for Kathy?"

Tom glanced at his sister, hearing her sarcasm, but Richard continued to beam happily. "She's about to marry society's most eligible bachelor, Liz. I love her, and I'll give her anything she wants."

"Is she expected to quit her job as Port Manager?"

"Of course not." Richard's smile was charming. "Hey, I'm a modern man!" He raised his binoculars to study the view. "Kathy told me a bit about the Japanese trawler, but no details. Why do you think those people chased you?"

As they told the story, Richard nodded sympathetically, then congratulated them. "You handled that well. But you forgot to mention — what did the signal say?"

Liz glanced at her brother. "Perhaps we're not supposed to tell. We'd better ask Kathy's permission."

"Fair enough," Richard said. "Listen, why not come over to my house tonight? You can meet Henry the parrot and I'll cook my famous spaghetti for everyone, including your Mom if she's not busy." He wrote down his address. "This is for your Mom. Kathy and I will collect you two from the Prescott Inn around seven."

"Sounds great," Tom said, and Liz nodded.

"I love making spaghetti because . . . ." Richard was interupted by a beeping sound. He went to the outside controls and picked up a cordless phone. "The *Quest* — Livingstone speaking."

Richard listened for a moment, then turned his back on Tom and Liz. Facing out to sea, he spoke briefly into the phone but his words were lost in the wind.

Then he hung up. "That was . . . that was my butcher! Yes, my butcher. He's got some steaks in from Alberta. I love that grain-fed beef!" Richard looked at his watch. "Time's going by, and I've got lots to do. See you tonight?"

"That'll be nice, Richard," Tom said. "Thanks!" As they left the schooner, and began walking along the dock, he grinned at Liz. "A chance to see Richard's old mansion! I can hardly . . . ."

Tom paused. Looking back at the schooner, he saw Richard Livingstone appear on deck. He'd quickly removed his foul weather gear, and now wore an overcoat that looked expensive, plus leather gloves and a colourful scarf. Hurrying across the dock, the man disappeared down a street between two office buildings.

"Let's see where's he going," Liz said.

They hurried forward. At the corner, Richard stood with impatient hands on his hips. He looked up and down the street, then checked his watch.

"I wonder who he's waiting for," Liz said.

"There's your answer," Tom replied, pointing at a black Citroen sedan coming down a hill. "Look who's driving!"

Liz shielded her eyes against the light. "It's that guy from Cape Spear. The one who told you to leave Newfoundland."

Tom nodded. "I still think he looks like a hawk. I bet

he's the one who phoned Richard at the schooner."

As they moved closer, the Citroen stopped. Richard jumped in, and the mud-splattered sedan pulled away. Tom ran forward, trying to see the licence plate, but it was too dirty. He watched the car continue up the street, then enter an undercover Parkade.

"Let's go see what happens." As they hurried along the street, Tom looked at Liz. "That Citroen's been driven on some muddy roads."

Inside the Parkade, the Austens followed a sloping ramp. Cars were parked to both sides, and steel doors led to exit stairways. Turning a corner, they saw the Citroen parked against a distant wall. The two men sat inside talking.

"The Hawk's window is open," Tom whispered. "Let's try to listen."

Keeping low, they moved closer. The men's voices could be heard, but not clearly. The air around Tom and Liz was dusty, tickling their noses. Finally only one car separated them from the Citroen. They crouched beside it, seeing their distorted faces in a chrome-plated hubcap.

Now Richard's voice was clear. "Stop worrying so much! Everything's going to be fine. Trust me, won't you?"

"But that boy in the barber shop . . . ."

"Relax, okay? There's only a few days left."

"But . . . ."

"I'm getting tired of your worrying. When I offered to help I didn't expect this!"

"But if I fail now. What a tragedy, after all . . . ."

"Stop it, please. Shape up, won't you? Be a man! Show some class!"

Kneeling on the concrete, Tom swiftly recorded the conversation in his notebook. The muffler hung down crookedly under the Citroen, and black oil dripped. They

heard a door open, then feet stepped down to the concrete. Tom recognized Richard's shoes and patterned
socks.

The Citroen's engine boomed in the concrete garage as
it reversed out of the space and drove away. Tom and Liz
looked at each other, then watched Richard's feet. The
man remained motionless until the Citroen had left the
Parkade. Then he laughed. "That fool," he chuckled.
"He's in for a surprise."

5

Liz stood at her window. Thunder crackled across the sky, and rain streamed down the glass. Tom was beside her. They were both crying sadly.

"The funeral will be in three days at Petty Harbour." Their mother sounded exhausted on the phone. "Are you getting enough to eat?"

"I guess so, but we feel horrible about Nanny. We'll try to have some spaghetti tonight, at Richard Livingstone's house. Remember, you're invited too." Liz said goodbye and hung up the phone. "I want to get moving, Tom. Let's leave a note on the front door for Richard and Kathy, saying we decided to walk. We can wait outside his house — the rain's stopping at last."

House lights gleamed from wet sidewalks as they crossed the city. As they walked, Tom and Liz wiped tears from their eyes as they talked about Nanny.

"Mom's going to need our help," Liz said.

Tom nodded.

"I wish Dad could get here. No news about those missing people in Arizona?"

Liz shook her head. "But he said on the phone last night they could be close to breaking the case."

"Great! Then he'll be here, and we can get his advice about that secret meeting between the Hawk and Richard. There's got to be a link to the Ice Diamond."

"Mom's too upset, we can't ask her." Liz looked up as dark clouds drifted across the moon. "Hey, see those houses and apartments ahead? Look at that huge sign. This is where Richard's going to build his park."

FUTURE HOME OF LIVINGSTONE PARK, the sign said. A PROUD GIFT TO A PROUD CITY. Two large pictures were on the sign — one featured Richard in colour, smiling. The second was in black and white. It showed a man with white hair and a determined face. He was handsome, with the rugged look of the outdoors, but his eyes weren't pleasant. They stared from the picture.

"That must be Richard's grandfather," Tom said. "The park is being built in his honour, remember?"

Liz nodded. "Those houses look nice. I got the impression from Richard they were falling apart."

Further up the street were some low-rise apartment buildings. They were also in good shape. Through the large windows they saw people eating supper, watching television, talking on the phone. "Those tenants have to get out. That'll be hard for them."

"Look on that balcony. Someone's hung a protest banner."

HANDS OFF MY HOME. I WANT TO STAY! was written on it

in black letters. Banners also hung from other balconies, and across some of the nearby houses. "Richard said these people want to leave," Tom said. "Then why the banners?"

Liz nodded. "It doesn't add up."

Reaching Waterford Bridge Road, they used Tom's map to find the side street where Richard's old family mansion stood, surrounded by trees, lawns and flower beds. The house was very dark, with no lights burning. There was a wide porch with a wooden roof, ancient stone walls and a round tower. Silver moonlight gleamed against the tower windows.

"A great place for ghosts," Liz said.

Tom nodded. "Richard and Kathy aren't here yet. Let's . . . ."

Liz grabbed his arm. "Look!"

Out of the night came the Jeep. As it turned into the side street, the headlights went out. Moving slowly, it pulled into the driveway of Richard's mansion and stopped in hiding behind a tall hedge. Moments later two figures in black ran swiftly across the lawn. At a ground-floor window they worked quickly with electrical tape and glass cutters. The crunch of breaking glass was followed by the sound of the window being raised.

"They're going inside," Tom said. "Come on!"

Moving forward from shadow to shadow, Tom and Liz were soon beside the house. They crept to the open window, and looked inside. They saw a dining room with a long table of polished wood and many chairs. Moonlight glowed through the window, showing a hallway with a staircase leading upstairs. On a table beside the staircase was a phone.

"We'd better call the police," Liz whispered. "Wait here, and I'll go inside."

"No way. I'm going with you."

Tom and Liz climbed through the window. Inside the dining room they tiptoed past the polished table into the hallway, where they listened for sounds.

Nothing.

Cautiously Liz raised the phone to her ear and began to call 911. Then she stopped. Leaning close to Tom she whispered, "The phone's dead."

He looked at the stairs. They curved gracefully to the next floor, where the glow of a flashlight came through an open door. Shadows moved on the wall. Tom and Liz started up — straight ahead was the open door. In the glare of the flashlight they saw the Renegades attaching explosives to a wall safe.

*   *   *

As the twosome took shelter behind a large desk, Tom and Liz lowered their heads. Seconds passed, then the air shook from the powerful explosion. As a bitter smell poured out of the room, Tom and Liz raised their heads to watch the Renegades search inside the safe.

"There's nothing here but cash and some jewellery," the woman said. "There's no birth certificate."

"The boss was sure Livingstone would hide the certificate in his safe."

"Sure, but it was just a guess. Maybe there isn't a certificate."

"Tell me again why we need it?"

"You've got a memory like a sieve," the woman muttered. "The boss found out the Ice Diamond is hidden where Livingstone's grandfather was born. If we'd found a birth certificate in the safe, it could have told us *where* he was born."

"Wasn't he born in a hospital?"

"No, you dolt! Lots of babies were born at home in the old days."

"This is a crazy job," the man growled. "Chasing kids around, breaking into a house and finding nothing. We shouldn't have taken this contract to find that Ice Diamond."

"The money's good," the woman replied. "You're the one who's always broke."

"Maybe so, but I still don't like it. This is a risky contract. We've been out of prison for three years now, and I never want to go back. Besides, what if we don't get paid?"

"No problem — we will."

"But you figure the Ice Diamond's worth a lot. What if we find the hiding place, then get cheated out of our share of the action?"

"No sweat," the woman said. "We'll get paid. It's all under control."

"Okay, but one more thing. Don't take me into any graveyards. I forgot how many old churches there are in the east. They spook me."

"How come?"

"I dunno. When I was a kid I went into some old stone churches, and I swear I felt ghosts around me. Don't laugh."

"I'm not!"

"Don't even smile."

"Lighten up," the woman said. "So you're scared of ghosts, big deal. Come on, let's take a final look and then get out of here. Livingstone's due home soon."

"Make it fast, okay?"

"Sure, sure," she replied. "I'm thinking maybe the birth certificate's hidden somewhere else in this office. It'll only take a minute to check around."

Liz touched Tom's arm and motioned. He followed her

down the stairs. "We can't let them escape," she whispered. "I've got a plan. Where's the kitchen, do you know?"

"Through that door."

Soon Liz was back, carrying a broom, which she pushed through the railing of the staircase. "It's a perfect height — exactly at ankle level." The broomstick stretched to the far side of the staircase. "Now let's yell."

Standing at the foot of the staircase, Tom and Liz shouted, "Help! Break-in! Help, police!"

There was a shout of surprise from the room upstairs. The Renegades' faces appeared in the gloom at the top of the staircase, then they saw Tom and Liz.

"It's those kids again! Let's get them!"

As the couple came swiftly down the dark staircase, the Austens darted away. Looking back, they saw the Renegades trip over the broomstick. They went down with terrible cries, hitting their heads against the wall and then the floor as they fell.

Running forward, Liz knelt over the couple. "They're knocked out, but I think they're okay. Let's phone the police from a neighbour's house."

"What if they wake up, and escape?" Tom hurried into the nearby dining room. "There's a big closet in here, Liz. We can lock them inside it."

Together they dragged the woman into the closet, then her partner. "Here's an extension cord," Liz said, pulling it out of a socket. "We can tie them together."

Within minutes, the couple was lying back-to-back inside the big closet with the cord wrapped around their arms. "Even if they wake up, they can't escape those knots," Liz said with satisfaction, as they closed the closet door and pushed a heavy chair against it. "Let's go phone the police."

Then a loud *squawk!* was heard, making Tom and Liz

jump. "What was that?" Liz said.

"It sounded like a parrot. Richard's got one, remember?"

"You're right! His name's Henry. Let's go see."

"Close the dining room door. If Henry's out of his cage, he could escape through that broken window."

The parrot was very loud, so they soon found him in the living room. "I bet he was upset by the noise when the Renegades fell," Tom said. He switched on a light. "Look at the beautiful feathers! All those colours."

The parrot had a large cage with several perches. He called *hello* in a raspy voice and bounced excitedly from perch to perch. As Tom went closer and grinned at Henry, car headlights swept the windows.

"That must be Richard and Kathy!" Liz said. "Come on, they can help with the Renegades!"

Tom and Liz hurried to the mansion's front door. As Richard opened Kathy's door he was laughing about something, but his laughter died when Tom and Liz blurted out the words *burglars!* and *break in!* He demanded details, anxious to know if the house and its contents were safe, then added, "Henry! Is the parrot safe?"

"Yes!"

"Thank goodness." Richard rushed away to the living room to check the parrot's safety, leaving Kathy to ask for details about the break-in. "Are those burglars still in the house? Did you actually see either of them?"

"Yes! It was that same man and woman who chased us to the trawler." Tom and Liz described what had happened, and pointed at the dining room. "They're tied up there, in a closet."

"Great work," Kathy said. "Congratulations! I'll check on them. You go get Richard and tell him to call the police. He's got a cellular phone in his car — he can use that."

"Great, because the phone line's been cut."

They found Richard in the kitchen, feeding treats to Henry. "His vocabulary's not bad," Richard said. "What's he said to you?"

"He said hello, really clearly. Richard, you've got to phone the police. You . . . ."

"That's all? Gee, that's too bad. Henry belongs to my son, who lives in Toronto now. When he left home Henry was moody but I've managed to cheer him up. Last week he said an entire sentence. I thought maybe . . . ."

Kathy rushed into the kitchen. "Tom and Liz, are you certain you left the Renegades in the dining room?"

"Yes."

She held up the extension cord. "You tied them with this?"

"Yes! But how. . . ."

"They've escaped. The dining room's empty."

*   *   *

Cold air blew in the broken window. The Renegades were gone. Then, in the shadow of a hedge, an engine roared and the Jeep raced out of hiding. The man and woman were inside.

"Who were they?" Richard said, watching the Jeep disappear into the night. "What did they want?"

Kathy looked at Tom and Liz. "When we came into the house I thought I smelled something bitter."

Tom nodded. "Explosives."

"Did those people you call the Renegades take anything from Richard's wall safe?"

Tom shook his head. "I don't think so."

"What were they after?" Richard said. "Do you know?"

"The hiding place for the Ice Diamond," Liz replied.

"What's that?"

"Oops." Liz glanced at Kathy. "Sorry, I guess that's a police secret. My mistake."

"No problem. Richard can be trusted, of course." Kathy quickly described the signal from sea, and what she knew about the Renegades. "They've got to be working for someone. The question is, who?"

"I've got enemies." Richard gazed out the broken window, looking sad. "People think Julius Ceasar had it bad. You could fill a phone book with the number of people who hate me."

Kathy gave him a sympathetic hug. "Sweetheart, why don't you phone the police? They should be setting up roadblocks to find that Jeep."

"No," Richard said. "Absolutely not. I don't want the police coming here. Nothing's been stolen, we'll just forget it. I can fix that broken window."

Liz looked at him. "The Renegades were after your grandfather's birth certificate."

"There isn't one," he said. "But I wonder why they wanted it?"

"They think the Ice Diamond's hidden where your grandfather was born."

"That's interesting," Kathy said. "Do you know where he was born, Richard?"

"Somewhere down the southern shore. Not far from Petty Harbour, actually, but I've no idea where."

"Is there an old family Bible?" Liz asked. "That's where people used to put that kind of information."

"I've never seen one." Richard turned to Tom and Liz. "Let me show you around. This is a fascinating old place."

After stopping at the office to check the damage to the safe Richard led them to the attic, where dusty sheets covered old furniture and the "steamer trunks" of his long-dead ancestors. "Solid oak," Richard said, booting one of the trunks. "Strong and everlasting, just like my family." He looked at Tom and Liz. "Want to see my grandfather's portrait? He's been dead many years. I loved the old guy, even if no one else did."

Downstairs in a book-lined den, Richard clicked on a small light over the fireplace. Yellow light showed an oil portrait in a gold-leaf frame. "Richard Livingstone the Second," he said proudly. "My grandfather."

It was the same man they'd seen on the billboard announcing Livingstone Park. This picture was in colour, painted in oils, but the face was still not pleasant.

Kathy glanced around the room. "Richard's fixed up this place like a little museum. Show Tom and Liz your proudest possession, sweetheart."

Richard walked over to a glass display case. Inside was an old lifejacket, grey with age. "This is actually from the *Titanic*. It sank not far from Newfoundland, you know. My great love is collecting artifacts. Anything about the history of Newfoundland. For example, the oil-skins I got for my schooner, or the famous black flag." He looked at the lifejacket. "This belonged to a small museum up the coast. Know how I got it?" He chuckled. "I bought the land the museum was sitting on. I told them to move the building because I was redeveloping the land. They were upset because they couldn't afford the move, so I made a deal. Give me the Titanic lifejacket, I said, and the land won't be developed." He laughed. "I never planned to develop it, anyway. It was just a clever way to get the lifejacket. These days it's priceless, of course."

Richard fed a biscuit to the parrot, who was perched on his shoulder. *"Foreclose,"* Henry squawked. *"Argggh! Develop!"*

Richard roared with laughter. "Isn't that great? It took

me months to teach him those words."

"I like these old photographs in the silver frames," Liz said.

"Those were taken by my grandfather from his plane — it was the first in Newfoundland."

Liz studied a faded black-and-white picture of seas pounding a cliff. A lighthouse stood at the top, and nearby, sheltered by trees, was a cabin. At the bottom of the cliff was a large cave, where a wooden dock had been built. Men were seen loading boxes into a small boat.

"Are they smugglers?" Tom asked.

Richard smiled. "No, those are miners. That cave led to a mine my grandfather owned. The ore was taken in those small boats to St. John's, for transfer to bigger ships. My grandfather made a lot of money from that mine. It's closed now."

"Was that his cabin on the cliff? Back in the woods?"

"Yes, it was beautiful when I last was there, as a child. Solid construction."

"What was the black flag you mentioned?"

"I'll show you." Richard opened a small wooden chest. "See that square of black silk? It was the great trophy of the sealing trade. Each year the ship bringing back the most seal pelts got to fly that silk. What a great way to generate hard work! The captains drove their men, determined to win the flag. The pelts came off the ice in the thousands, and the Livingstones grew rich. We had a huge fleet, and so did the other owners. Those were the days."

"I've been reading *Death on the Ice,*" Tom said. "It sounds rough out there."

"Our sealers were the best, Tom. The best! They loved it out on the ice, what a challenge! Besides, they had their families to feed."

"Was it good pay? In the book, she says . . . ."

"Hey, Tom, you're my guest! I don't want to argue sealing with you." He gave Tom's shoulder a friendly squeeze. "Come on, let's have some spaghetti, then maybe Kathy can drive you home. I really appreciate your help tonight, capturing that couple and everything."

"But," Liz said, "how did the Renegades escape?" Her face was puzzled. "I know they couldn't have reached my knots, so someone else untied them."

"Obviously someone came in that broken window," Kathy said.

"Tell you what," Richard said. "Let's get some spaghetti cooking, then I'll check again for a housebreaker. My food's still the best in town."

"Sounds great," Tom said. "I'm famished!"

*　　　*　　　*

Later that evening Kathy drove them home. "I've been working long hours," she said, yawning. "I'm under a lot of pressure right now."

"Kathy," Liz asked, "why the break-in at Richard's? Any theories?"

"Not really, although it's true Richard has some enemies. But it sounds like those Renegades were after information. Maybe someone wants to blackmail him."

"I don't think so," Liz said. "Those Renegades only talked about finding the hiding place for the Ice Diamond." She hesitated, then said, "Kathy, does Richard hold many meetings in the downtown Parkade?" When Kathy looked surprised, Liz explained what she meant. Then she asked, "Have you ever met that man? The one we call the Hawk?"

Kathy shook her head. "You think he's also connected to the Ice Diamond? I'd better ask Richard some more questions. I'm getting more and more worried for him.

Richard thinks he's strong, but he's not. Something strange is happening, and I'm afraid he'll get hurt."

*   *   *

The next day was perfect for winter sailing. The wind came off the grey Atlantic in cold gusts, but Tom and Liz were wearing foul-weather gear that felt cozy as they walked down to the harbour. Earlier that morning a messenger had delivered woolen toques called watch caps, deck boots and one-piece jumpsuits with thermal protection, all courtesy of Livingstone Sea Profits.

The schooner waited by the dock, its flags cracking in the strong wind. Richard was busy on deck, but he stopped working as Tom and Liz approached.

"Glad you could make it! Kathy hasn't arrived yet."

"I see Henry's going with us," Tom said, putting down the lunch he'd brought along.

"You bet!" Richard glanced at the parrot on his shoulder. "Say good morning."

"Morning! Arrgh! Have a nice day!" Looking pleased, Richard gave Henry a treat. With a swallow, the biscuit disappeared. *"Arrgh! Pieces of eight."*

"I taught him to say that." Richard smiled proudly. "Tourists expect pirate talk from a parrot."

"We saw where Livingstone Park is going to be built," Liz said. "Those houses and apartments look quite nice."

"They're okay, I suppose, but Livingstone Villas will be a much better place to live. Everything will be brand-new. No taps to fix, no walls to repaint, no old carpeting that needs changing. Think of that!"

"Where's it going to be?"

"A real nice place in the country. A bit far from town maybe, but I'll sponsor a shuttle bus."

"Couldn't the tenants fix up their places?" Liz asked.

"They had protest banners saying they wanted to stay. I felt upset for them."

Tom nodded. "Me too."

"They'll love their new homes, once they've moved. People don't like change in their lives, but that's the price of progress." Richard studied their faces. "You may go into business some day. You'll want to be a success, so here's what I learned from my grandfather. Work hard, pay for the best advice, and always look out for Number One. If you must be ruthless to people, be swift. Don't give them time to prepare a defence."

"But," Liz said, "I'm not sure . . . ."

"Ever heard of W.C. Fields? A great actor, one of the best. He once said, "never give a sucker an even break." Excellent advice, and here's something else — remember that big government is bad government." He stared at them. "Government must be lean and stream-lined. Get rid of welfare, and end unemployment insurance. People need to work for a living. They need pride. That's what my grandfather always said."

Tom looked at him. "I . . . ."

"If I'm a wealthy man, why should I pay for a poor person to go into hospital? That's how taxes are wasted. Let the poor person get a job and pay hospital bills that way. It's not fair to make me pay for someone else."

"But maybe that sick person can't find work," Tom protested, "or has been hurt in an accident. That's why the government helps out."

Richard laughed. "Hey, another discussion! Come on kids, I'll teach you the power controls for the *Quest*. You'll be sailors in no time. By the way, you look fabulous in that gear. Good enough to pose for an ad."

"Thanks," Liz said. "You were nice to arrange it."

Tom nodded. "By the way, why did you call your boat the *Quest?*"

"My parents died tragically when I was young."
Richard replied. "My grandfather taught me that life is a
series of quests. Always search for a new goal, a fresh
challenge. This schooner is my latest search for success."

Going to the railing that overlooked the water, Richard
studied Cabot Tower with his binoculars. "I should build
another tower up there, in honour of my family."

"I've been thinking about last night's break-in," Tom
said. "I think it's really important to find your grandfather's birth place before those Renegades do. Is there
anywhere else we could search for information?"

Richard shook his head. "I don't think so."

"I've got an idea," Liz said. "You said he grew up near
Petty Harbour, so we could check the church there.
Maybe they've got some old records — you know, births,
baptisms, marriages, that kind of thing."

"Good idea," Tom exclaimed. "If we find the records
for your grandfather, Richard, they could easily give the
exact place where he was born."

He nodded. "Maybe . . . ."

Suddenly Richard turned, and stared across the deck of
the schooner. Standing at the top of the gangplank were
Kathy and her secretary, Dave Foster. "What are you
doing here?" Richard shouted.

"I'm going sailing with you, sweetheart," Kathy said.
"You know that."

"Not you, Kathy. *Him!*" Richard pointed an angry fin-
ger at Dave Foster. "I know you're in love with Kathy,
but she's mine. Get that, Foster? She's *mine,* so get off
my boat."

The handsome, white-haired man shrugged. "Okay, if
that's what you want. I was hoping we could be a bit
more friendly."

He glanced at Kathy, then went down the gangplank
shaking his head. Richard waited until he'd driven away

in his fancy car, then turned to Kathy. "Did Foster hear me talking to the kids about Grandfather's birth records?"

"Sure, sweetheart. You've got a loud voice, but don't worry about Dave. He can be trusted."

"Nobody can be trusted," Richard scowled. As he cast off the lines his brow remained furrowed, and a nerve jumped in his forehead. "We'll use the engine until we leave the harbour," he told Tom and Liz. "I'll teach you these outside power controls, and the wheel. Later we'll go below deck, and you can try the controls inside the bubble."

Waves began slapping the hull as the *Quest* moved away from the dock. The wind became stronger, and it felt good on their faces. Tom and Liz quickly mastered the controls and took the *Quest* smoothly between the high cliffs of the Narrows. Far above was the Cabot Tower.

"You kids learn fast," Richard said, "but I think I'll take over now. We're on the open sea."

"Is that Cape Spear ahead in the distance?"

"Yes. We'll pass it, heading south."

"Is Petty Harbour a long way?"

"Nope. It's about a half hour drive by land."

"Mom's going down in the Chev," Liz told Kathy. "We'll meet her at Petty Harbour. It'll be nice to see our relatives. My cousin Sarah is 16, like me, and Duncan's ten."

Kathy looked at Tom. "How old are you?"

"Fourteen."

"Oh to be young again," Kathy said, smiling at Richard. Turning to Liz, she pulled out a copy of *People*. "Look who's the cover story this week."

"The mystery prince!" Liz leaned over the article, zooming through the pictures and story. "The threat to his life is really serious. That's because the Prince will probably try to get his country back when he turns 18 in a few days." She looked at Tom. "The country is still controlled by the revolutionaries. If the Prince returns, they could lose everything."

"So there's a price on his head," Kathy said. "The revolutionaries want the Prince dead. They've offered a lot of money to anyone who finds him."

"Quit gossiping," Richard said. "I've got problems of my own, Kathy. I need a sympathetic ear."

"What's the problem, sweetheart?"

"I had a radio message from Petty Harbour. There may be a demonstration when we arrive. That woman is stirring up trouble again."

"Ginger Watson?"

Richard nodded. "She doesn't want the schooner docking at Petty Harbour."

"Why?" Tom asked.

"Just because I'm a Livingstone."

Tom looked at the open Atlantic. It was huge and empty, stretching away until the blue water finally met the pale blue sky. "It's so lonely out here. Remember the teenage sealer who owned that oilskin? I keep thinking about him, sailing out of the Narrows just like us. How did he feel, heading for the ice? Homesick and scared, I bet."

"I doubt it," Richard said. "Sealing was a great adventure."

"But in that book it sounds horrible. The author said the ice wasn't solid. The sealers jumped from floe to floe, and some guys fell between and drowned." Tom shivered. "It freaks me."

"Okay to go below and have something to eat?" Tom asked, picking up his lunch. "Maybe I'll feel better then."

"Sure thing, Tom. You going, Liz?"

She shook her head. "I'm hoping to try the controls again. It's really fun."

Richard smiled. "That might be possible."

Tom opened the door beside the wheel. "See you later." Going down the narrow stairs into the cabin, he looked at the lamps swinging from the low beams above. Steadying himself, Tom crossed the cabin to the oilskins. Searching through them, he found the one with the name Hunter inside. Tom thought for a moment about the teenage sealer, then decided to try the oilskin on.

It felt strange, and he was tempted to get rid of it. But instead he sat down on a wooden bunk, took out a sandwich, and leaned against the hull. Opening *Death on the Ice,* he began to read.

After a while Tom's eyes became heavy. Stretching out on the rough lumber, he cradled his head on his arms. Images from the book crossed his mind. He thought of the sealers, huddled around a stove below decks before going on the ice, and he tried to imagine the teenager named Hunter. What did he look like? What were his feelings going out to the ice? Tom thought of the frozen floes, growling and shifting beneath the boy's boots.

Before long, Tom slept.

6

"Boy, on your feet. We're going to the ice."

A big, bearded man in oilskins stood over the bunk. Tom's eyelids felt stiff. He sat up slowly. "What's that noise?"

"The ice grinding against the hull."

Teenagers and men in oilskins and leather boots were huddled around the stove. "Have a mug-up, boy," one said. "Black tea and molasses. You'll be needing the energy out on the ice."

On deck, the sunlight was blinding. It glittered from the pack ice that growled against the schooner. The frozen wilderness was everywhere. Sealers were already on the ice, jumping from floe to floe. Scrambling off the schooner, Tom looked at the wheelhouse. *Standing beside the whiskered Captain was a man he'd seen somewhere before. His eyes were fierce under bushy brows. Big arms were crossed over his powerful chest.*

"Who's that?"

"His company's called Livingstone Sea Profits," the old sealer replied. "He owns this boat, and many more. He's building a mansion at St. John's. Keep moving, boy." *The sealer jumped to another floe. The ice wobbled under his feet.* "Livingstone would squeeze gold from rocks with his bare hands, if he could."

Suddenly a teenage boy shouted as the ice parted and he fell through. Others grabbed him in time, but his leather boots had filled with icy water.

"Sir!" *One of the sealers looked at the owner, watching from the schooner.* "Let James have dry boots. His feet are soaked."

The owner shook his head. "There are no boots. I do not provide them."

James squeezed water from the leather. "Please, sir," *he called.* "Let me dry beside the stove, then join the others."

"No. I need you on the ice. How else does this company make money?"

The boy pulled on his damp boots, and faced the ice floes again. The others went with him.

"They're not even arguing!" *Tom looked in astonishment at the owner.* "He won so easily. Why don't the sealers quit?"

The man beside him shook his head. "How would their families eat?"

"Unemployment insurance, or welfare. The government would help them."

He shook his head. "These sealers have no such protection. Their choice is simple. Be a slave to Livingstone, *or watch your family starve. Which would you choose?"*

Tom looked at a distant mountain of ice crystals, piled high. The sun sparkled from its jagged pinnacles. A trail of men from other schooners was moving toward the ice mountain, searching for seals. He moved forward with the bearded man, struggling across the ice as it moved and shifted. Then the sealer raised his head. "A storm's blowing up. Now the weather will drop right out."

Snow devils whirled across the frozen white wilderness. Ice pans growled against each other, and the floe beneath Tom's feet rocked alarmingly. A bitter wind cut through the oilskin he wore. "Let's return on board!" The wind was shrieking so loudly, Tom had to yell. "Where's the ship gone? I can't see it!"

"The captain sailed away, boy. He may return tomorrow, or maybe the next day. He's some anxious to find the most seals, so he needs men searching everywhere. He wants to win that black flag."

"Will his men get extra money if they win?"

The sealer shook his head. Then he looked down at the ice floe. "Feel the sea swelling beneath us." Suddenly the sky closed around them. Wet snow flakes landed on their skin, clinging. "We're lost, boy. Down on your knees and pray. It's our only hope now."

Tom shielded his eyes against the snow. "Look! Other sealers, coming our way. They're in trouble!"

Six men were struggling together across the ice. Two of them crawled, leaving a trail of blood from their torn knees; the others stumbled forward on frozen feet. Their faces were white with frost. Some had bare hands frozen into shapes like claws. "A warm stove," one called in a frail voice. "Help us."

The sealers staggered closer. Tom reached out his

hands to them, trying to help. He groaned. He was so cold.

"Tom, wake up!"

Liz leaned over him. "You've been having a nightmare. I came into the cabin, and you were moaning."

Tom sat up, struggling out of the oilskin. "Help me get this off!"

"What's wrong?" Liz said.

"It belonged to that teenage sealer named Hunter. I just had a dream, like I was him." Tom shuddered. "What a horrible experience. I'll tell you about it later — I need some air."

As they opened the cabin door, Liz said, "I love this schooner! I've been at the wheel, learning how to manoeuvre in heavy seas."

"It's windy!" Stepping on deck, Tom grabbed a handrail. The schooner rose up on a foaming grey wave, then plunged down into the surging seas. The skies above were angry; along the foot of the nearby cliffs the sea crashed ashore, throwing white water high in the air.

Richard was at the wheel, steering with one hand as he watched the sails handle the wind. "This is living," he shouted. "I'm a happy man. Come on, Liz, try the helm again. Then Tom."

Kathy grinned. "Richard, sometimes you're almost a fun guy. If only you didn't think about money all the time. Then I could really love you."

"Watch out," Tom yelled, as a huge wave came at the *Quest* with the power of a freight train. But the schooner handled it beautifully, riding easily over the surging wave as spray lashed their faces. Richard shook seawater from his hair, then grinned at Tom. "Your sister's a great sailor! You want to try the helm now?"

Tom shook his head. "No thanks, Richard."

"You look sad," Kathy said. "You've probably been

thinking about your grandmother. Mine died a year ago, and I felt rotten."

Tom nodded. "Sometimes I'm afraid I'll never get over it."

"You will," Kathy said, "and you know the good thing? Because you've experienced deep grief, you'll be able to feel great joy when it comes to you." She hugged his shoulders. "Your emotions are getting stretched, Tom. That's growth, and it's always a good thing in the end."

"Thanks, Kathy," Tom said quietly. He looked down the coast. Waves smashed against the cliffs for a long distance. "How far to Petty Harbour?"

"We're almost there," Richard replied, taking over the helm from Liz. "It's tucked behind the cliff we're just approaching. Ten minutes maximum. Feeling seasick?"

Tom shook his head. "It's nice of you to sail us down, Richard. Are you returning to St. John's today?"

"No, I'm hoping to stay in Petty Harbour a few days. I think the locals will enjoy having the schooner around to look at."

"But you said there could be a demonstration," Liz said. "What about?"

Richard's eyes narrowed. "A woman named Ginger Watson lives in Petty Harbour. She's my enemy. She's always protesting against me. Whenever there's a demonstration outside my office I know I'll see Ginger carrying the biggest sign."

"Why's she so upset?" Liz asked.

Richard took the *Quest* safely over another big wave. "Unfortunately, some members of her family died on the ice. Sealing lasted until quite recently, you know. My family still had men on the ice when I was a kid. There were deaths every year, of course, but it was a hazardous job. Among the last to die were Ginger's two brothers and her Dad. Because of that she carries a grudge against the name Livingstone."

"Are you worried about the demonstration?" Tom asked.

"No, but I don't like it. I'm a quiet man. I just want to spend a few days in Petty Harbour then go home, but Ginger will try to prevent it. She's not a fair person." Richard frowned. "Our company had a lot of bad publicity the winter Ginger's family died on the ice. There were two tragedies, both caused by foolish mistakes. In a way, Livingstone Sea Profits has never recovered from the negative media coverage. We've got balance-sheet problems to this day, and I hold people like Ginger Watson to blame for that."

Kathy squeezed his hand.

"My son left home because of her," Richard said. His voice was bitter. "I was raising him as the company's next president so I could retire and do some travelling. Instead, Ginger Watson's bad publicity turned my son off the business. He left for Toronto. I haven't seen him since."

"I'm sorry," Liz said. "That's really sad."

Richard smiled. "Hey, let's cheer up! I see Petty Harbour ahead."

Between two cliffs, the sea ran into a narrow harbour. Hills rose on both sides of the water. Long ago a glacier had passed over the rugged landscape, leaving behind slabs of rock. Built among the rocks were homes of many bright colours, each appearing to face a different direction.

Richard skillfully guided the *Quest* closer to the harbour mouth. "You see the breakwater?" He pointed toward a large structure built across the harbour entrance. In the middle was an opening for boats to pass through. "That opening's called the Notch," Richard explained. "The breakwater protects the boats inside from heavy seas. Petty Harbour faces due east, straight into the Atlantic."

"It's been a fishing village for four hundred years," Kathy said. "I've heard they still use the same basic methods, helped by modern technology. Great, eh?"

Waves slapped heavily against the breakwater as the *Quest* approached, but the schooner slipped easily through the Notch into calm waters. Manouevering expertly, Richard soon had the boat moored safely against the breakwater's inside wall. He called his thanks to the local teenagers who'd helped with the lines, then he frowned.

A woman had appeared on the doorstep of a small house nearby. About sixty, with curly grey hair and blue eyes, she wore jeans and a parka.

At her mouth was a power megaphone.

"He's arrived," cried her amplified voice. *"Everyone down to the breakwater. Fast!"*

*   *   *

Other doors opened immediately and people came out. They wore winter clothes; some carried protest signs. As they walked down the hill to the breakwater, Richard turned his back and began casually drying the schooner's brass fixtures with a cloth.

"Richard Livingstone," Ginger Watson's voice boomed as she stepped onto the breakwater. *"You . . . ."*

Richard silenced her with an angry gesture. "Turn that thing off, Miss Watson! Your own voice is loud enough."

She lowered the megaphone. Her blue eyes had the colour and strength of cobalt. For a moment she stared at Richard, then said, "You're asking for trouble, Mr. Livingstone. Why have you come here?"

"Because I'm proud of my new schooner, and I want you all to see it."

"Rubbish. You've come for some crooked reason. I can feel it in my bones."

Richard laughed. "You're not a detective, Miss Watson."

"Maybe so, but I know you're not wanted in Petty Harbour."

A woman behind her spoke, "Wait a minute, Ginger. You know we don't all agree with you. Not everyone here lost men on the ice. This is an open harbour. Your anger is no reason to deny shelter to Mr. Livingstone's schooner."

"But, he's one of the pirates of Water Street!" Ginger protested. "Those sealing companies made slaves of our men. They paid them almost nothing to go on to the ice and maybe die!" She paused, struggling to stay calm. "My poor father was past the age of retirement. He was tired. He wanted to stay home, and rest. But our family had no savings, so father had to remain a sealer. *He died out there!*"

Richard raised both hands. "Miss Watson, you know I'm sorry about that. I've phoned you, I've written you, my company has even sent you money."

"Only to buy my silence, and stop me protesting! I tore your money into shreds."

"What more can I do?" Richard looked at the local people standing along the breakwater. "Are you all against me, too?"

"No," a man said. The lines on his face revealed a lifetime at sea in open boats. "You're welcome to the shelter of our harbour."

"That's right," his wife agreed. She looked nice and had short hair, turning grey. "But you are not invited to Sunday dinner, Mr. Livingstone. We haven't forgotten the truth about the pirates of Water Street. The sealing companies stole our men's pride. They stole their dignity."

"I don't know what you mean."

The man stared at him. "Never been poor, Mr. Livingstone? Never go to school without a lunch when you were a kid? Never wear shoes that filled with rainwater because your family couldn't afford new soles?"

"Maybe not, but . . . ."

"You were on television last week, Mr. Livingstone. Barbara Frum asked the secret of your self-confidence. You said you're always looking out for Number One."

"What's wrong with that?"

The man stepped closer. The hair above his forehead was thin, and flecked with grey. He curled his big hand into a fist.

"You only believe in yourself, Richard Livingstone. You're just like your grandfather. You keep people poor, because it suits your purposes. People who work for low wages are busy just trying to live so they haven't the energy to struggle against you. Then your friends get into politics and take over the government. They pass laws that you like. Cut back on welfare, close the women's shelters, reduce money for education. Hurt all the people without power, just so you can pay smaller taxes and have more money for steaks and expensive cars."

He took his wife's hand. "So, Mr. Livingstone, you can have the shelter of our harbour. But you won't be seated at the supper table when my family prays this Sunday."

The man and his wife walked away together. As they did, Ginger Watson and many others followed. But some remained to study the schooner and ask Richard questions.

Looking up the hillside, Tom and Liz saw their mother's Chev arrive outside a yellow house. A second car also pulled to a stop. "There's our cousins and their parents," Liz said to Kathy. "They drove out to the highway, to meet Mom." She waved at the boy and girl, then watched them run down the hill toward the breakwater. "We'll be staying with Sarah and Duncan. Nanny was their grandmother, too."

"I'm sorry about her," Kathy said. "I'll be coming to the funeral with Richard. My secretary, Dave Foster, also wants to be there."

"Are you returning to the city today, Kathy?"

"I'm not sure. I feel like keeping an eye on Richard." She paused, looking at him on deck answering questions. "Richard's got more enemies than he realizes, and I'm worried."

*   *   *

Moments later, the cousins reached the breakwater. Sarah was the same age as Liz, with red hair pulled back in a thick ponytail. She had pretty eyes, and looked friendly. Beside her stood Duncan. He and Tom could have been brothers with their vivid red hair and multitude of freckles. Their blue eyes were the same, and they liked each other immediately.

After saying goodbye to Kathy and Richard, the four cousins left the breakwater. "It's great to meet Tom and Liz Austen," Duncan said. "My friends want autographs."

"Sure," Tom said. "I bet."

"But only if they're free." Duncan grinned. "Have you been screeched in yet?"

"No, but what . . . ."

Duncan turned a delighted face to Sarah. "They haven't been screeched in! What luck!"

"What's going on?" Liz asked. "What's that mean?"

Sarah smiled. "You'll find out. It's a Newfoundland ceremony, kind of an official welcome." She turned to her brother. "It's a bit different, right?"

"You bet!" He looked at Tom. "What did you think about the signal I spotted?"

"That was great, Duncan! Have you seen the yacht again?"

"Only once, but that gave me a pattern. According to my calculations, it will return tonight at 21:00 hours. I'm hoping it'll be visible again from Spyglass Hill." Duncan looked at Liz. "You and Tom coming to the hill tonight?"

"I guess so!"

At the end of the breakwater, Tom took a picture of a dock piled high with salty-smelling nets. Next to them were huge red floats that looked like the eggs of alien creatures. The hills beyond were misty grey.

"I love your houses," Liz said. "It looks like people built them wherever they found a flat space."

"That's right," Sarah said. "I can't wait to show you around. I think you'll like my friends."

Liz sighed. "Too bad we're here because of losing our Nanny."

"We all loved her so much," Sarah said. "Just about the entire village will come to the house in the next couple of days to pay their respects, and share some stories."

"We call our village the Harbour," Duncan told Tom. He waited a moment, then said, "Aren't you going to write that in your notebook?"

"How'd you know about my notebook?"

"Because you're Tom Austen!" Duncan's face glowed. "I can't wait to show you and Liz my detective agency. My office is in the basement of our house. It gets kind of cold in winter, but nobody ever said a gumshoe's life is easy." He turned to Liz. "What's your toughest case so far?"

"Green Gables was really hard on my nerves, but that's where I met my friend Makiko from Japan. I'm going to New Brunswick next summer, and Makiko's meeting me there. It'll be great to see her again."

Duncan looked at Tom. "And your toughest case?"

"The one on the train — I was a beginner then. I had lots to learn."

"So anyway," Duncan said, "what's your theory about the Ice Diamond?"

"Is there buried treasure around here?" Tom asked.

"You mean like Oak Island? Where you and Liz saw EVEL scratched in the dirt? Maybe that's the answer — someone's after buried pieces of eight!"

"What do people in the Harbour think about the signal?" Tom asked.

Duncan sighed. "I've been asking questions, but nobody takes me seriously. For two years I've pestered people for a case to solve. Missing car keys, anything. Everyone knows I'm desperate for a mystery, so they think I dreamed up the signal."

"Didn't anyone else see it?"

Duncan shook his head. "There's no fishing right now, so the boats aren't out. Both nights I saw the yacht it was stormy, so people had their curtains pulled. I'm the only one who saw the signal."

"I believe my brother," Sarah said. "That's why I'm going with him tonight, to see the signal with my own eyes."

"We haven't been able to talk to Mom and Dad about it," Duncan said. "They've been really upset about Nanny, and now they're preparing for the Wake."

"What's that?" Tom asked.

"For three days people will visit to talk about Nanny, and share our feelings. People talk and laugh, it's a really nice time. That's called a Wake, then there's the funeral."

Duncan watched Tom focus his camera on fishing boats tied to a wharf. "Anyway, about the Ice Diamond. I've been searching Petty Harbour for a hiding place, but no luck." A seagull drifted out of the mist, then its pink feet touched down on the roof of a large wooden shed. "That's called a stage. They're for storing nets and other fishing gear."

"Could the Ice Diamond be hidden in a stage?" Tom asked.

Duncan shook his head. "I've checked them all, top to bottom."

Sarah looked at Liz. "Ginger Watson hates Richard, because of her family's menfolk dying on the ice, but isn't he handsome? Imagine actually sailing on his schooner, you lucky things! What's it like?"

"It's different, all right," Liz said. "So's Richard."

At a corner confectionary they bought something to eat, then began to climb a narrow road. Two men working under the hood of a pickup called *G'day,* and a woman smiled from her yard. "Newfoundland people are so friendly," Tom said, as a child waved from a porch. "The Harbour's a neat place. Is there much crime?"

Sarah shook her head. "The nearest police station is at Mount Pearl, way over at St. John's. People leave their doors unlocked. They trust each other."

Near the top of the steep hill they reached the house. There were lobster traps in the yard, and Duncan's bicycle leaned against the front steps. A beagle ran back and forth inside a large wire enclosure containing a dog house.

"That's our pup Frisky," Duncan said. "Come meet him."

Tom and Liz hugged the energetic puppy, then went inside. A lot of people were visiting, and many were crowded into the huge kitchen. Mrs. Austen kissed Tom and Liz, asked about the schooner trip, then turned to a bright-eyed woman beside her.

"This is your great-great Aunt Millie."

"It's good to meet you," she said, kissing them. Her skin was dry and light, like paper. "I'm the oldest in our family, but not in the Harbour. Lucy Chalmers is 87. She's away in Labrador, visiting her family. You'll meet her at the funeral." She studied Liz. "I understand you're the superstitious one. The top fell off a pot today, as I cooked. Know what that meant?"

"No, Aunt Millie."

"That we'd be having visitors." Smiling, she looked at the people jammed into the kitchen. "But that was easy to predict. All these guests are a wonderful tribute to your grandmother. And just imagine — you've come all the way from Winnipeg."

"We're glad to be here."

"Been screeched in?"

"No, and . . . ."

"Oh boy!" Aunt Millie clapped her hands. "I can't wait!" She whispered in the ear of a woman beside her, who also clapped her hands. Tom exchanged a worried look with his sister, then looked around the kitchen. It had a big stove, comfortable chairs and a large TV set. On the walls were many school pictures, including those of Tom and Liz. Nearby was a photo of a boat.

"My Dad built that longliner," Duncan said proudly. "Come say hi to my folks."

In the next room Tom and Liz met their aunt and uncle, who both had red hair and freckles. In their uncle's arms was a tiny baby. "This is Samantha, my new sister," Duncan said proudly. "Finally I'm not the youngest in the family."

Liz blew a kiss at Samantha. "For good luck," she

explained. "Makiko said people in the Orient do that with newborns."

Sarah arrived with some drinks. "We call this syrup," she said. "It's made in St. John's, by a company called Purity. It's some good."

"You're right," Tom said, as he swallowed the delicious drink. "What's the food like here?"

"Great!" Duncan said. "We'll serve you fish faces for sure."

"Fish what?"

"Cod heads! The tongues are like jelly." As Tom and Liz turned pale Duncan laughed. "Or how about some scrunchions? That's bits of fried pig. We'll probably have scrunchions tonight."

Sarah shook her head. "We're having salmon, Duncan. Why don't you show Tom your office? Liz and I are going to my room, to talk."

*   *   *

Duncan's office was a tribute to the great detectives. On the bookshelves stood authors like Sir Arthur Conan Doyle and Agatha Christie, and reference texts with titles like *The Private Investigator's Basic Manual*. A movie poster showed Humphrey Bogart in search of the Maltese falcon, and another advertised the classic *Dr. Jekyll and Mr. Hyde*.

Duncan dropped down in a dusty armchair and rested his feet on a wooden crate. In front of him, the wall was painted with a fake fireplace. "That's sort of like Sherlock Holmes," he explained. "This is where I think. Pull up a chair, and settle."

Tom took a chair from the small desk and sat beside his cousin. "What are those old clothes in the closet? Disguises?"

"I guess so, if I ever get a good case. Right now they're for mummering."

"What's that?"

"It's a Newfoundland tradition. In November everyone dresses in weird outfits, and goes house to house. We call it mummering."

"It's sort of like Halloween?"

"A bit, but parents dress up, too. We visit a house and have lots to eat, and some dancing and singing, then move on to the next place."

"Sounds great. Why's it called mummering?"

Duncan thought for a moment. "You know, I can't say."

"Ever seen real seals out on the ice?"

"Sure. Dad took us out in the boat. They bark really loud, and try to hide behind chunks of ice. A polar bear came ashore near here, that was some sight. I've decided to be a wildlife officer when I'm older. But listen, how do you like Newfoundland?"

"It's a wonderful place. I'm proud these are my roots."

Duncan grinned. "I almost forgot. It's time for you to be screeched in."

7

Upstairs, the house was jammed with people. They stood in hallways and every room, talking and laughing as they remembered Nanny's life. Mrs. Austen was talking to a woman in a beautifully styled black dress. Her dark hair was held in place by a patterned black headband.

"Aunt Melody," Tom said in surprise. "I didn't think you'd be coming to the funeral. Aren't you performing with an opera in Madrid?"

"My Spanish understudy is going to play the role while I'm away, Tom."

"You look wonderful, Aunt Melody. You've become a real success in the opera. Congratulations."

"Thanks!" She hugged him, then turned to Duncan.

"You've grown so much, Duncan. I hardly recognize you."

"You don't come home enough, Aunt Melody, but I guess that's the price of fame." He smiled. "Guess what? Tom and Liz are going to be screeched in, right now."

"Wonderful!" Aunt Melody's large dark eyes widened happily. "I arrived just in time."

Duncan led them into the big kitchen where people were jammed in together. Aunt Millie and Liz were busy with a kettle and mugs. "I'm teaching Liz to make Lassy Tea," Aunt Millie said to Tom, holding up a jar. "The secret is this brand of molasses, and lots of it. Lassy tea's kept me healthy all these years."

Duncan called for attention. "Good news," he said, as heads turned. "Two mainlanders are with us tonight. They haven't been screeched in."

A cheer shook the room. All eyes went to Tom and Liz. No one spoke, but everyone was smiling. Tom watched Duncan go into the utility room. He opened a freezer, and lifted out a large frozen fish.

"That's a cod," Liz said. "We studied them in school."

"Why's Duncan bringing it in here?"

"I don't want to know."

With Sarah at his side, Duncan carried the cod forward. Its mouth was slightly open, and the eyes were blank. There was frost on its frozen body.

"Down on your knees," Duncan ordered.

Tom knelt beside Liz. The fish was directly in front of his eyes. Up close, it was really ugly. He looked up at Duncan. His cousin was smiling.

"Now," Duncan said, "kiss the cod."

"*What?*"

"Kiss it. On the lips."

Tom groaned, then glanced at his sister. "You go first."

"No way."

Sarah looked down at them. "Tom, you're first."

Closing his eyes, he quickly kissed the frozen cod. As Liz took her turn, Tom wiped his mouth.

"Yuck! Is the ceremony over?"

Sarah shook her head. Taking a bottle from a cupboard, she poured dark liquid into two cups. "This is cod liver oil," she said. "Drink it."

They got it down, but the taste was horrible.

"It'll be gone in a day or two," Duncan said. "Now stand, and recite these words after me: *I shall forever honour this fair island known as The Rock.* This completes your official welcome to Newfoundland."

When the pledge was over, people crowded around with laughter and congratulations. Tom and Liz swallowed water, trying to clean their mouths, then heard the chimes of a big clock announcing the hour.

"21:00 hours," Duncan said. "The yacht is due back. It's time to climb Spyglass Hill."

*   *   *

Outside, the wind was blowing. On the dark hills, the windows of houses glowed. The waters of the narrow harbour reflected the headlights of occasional cars. Using Duncan's spyglass, Tom studied the village. At the breakwater, Richard Livingstone sat alone on the deck of his schooner, staring out to sea.

"Kathy's gone back to the city," Tom said. "Richard must be lonely."

Liz turned to Sarah. "I think he's really jealous of Kathy's secretary, Dave Foster. He wears some pretty fancy Italian styles."

"Those clothes are expensive," Sarah said. "Maybe Mr. Foster wants to find the Ice Diamond. He could sell it to a jeweller, and get some big money."

They climbed a narrow path up Spyglass Hill. "The stars are so bright," Liz exclaimed. "Ever wonder what's up there?"

Sarah nodded. "I want to be an astronaut, or an expert on the planets."

"Every star is a sun. Think of the hundreds of planets out in space! Is there another one like Earth? I'd love to know."

High on the hill, they looked out to sea. Waves boomed against the cliffs, driven by the wind. Duncan lifted the spyglass — its brass was very old. "This was Poppy's. He left it to me when he died."

"Do you come up here a lot?" Liz asked.

Duncan nodded. "It's my special place. The night I first saw the yacht I was up here, crying. Nanny had just gone into the hospital."

Hugging him, Liz brushed away a tear. "We all loved her so much."

For a moment they were quiet. Then Duncan said, "Want to try my spyglass?"

"Sure!"

As Liz knelt, studying the sea, the others were silent. Then Sarah asked, "Heard about that mystery prince?"

"You bet," Liz said. "His 18th birthday is Tuesday. That's when he can claim his country back."

"Unless bounty hunters catch him first. There's a big price on his head."

"Did you hear he'll inherit 34 titles? Defender of the Realm, Sun King, Commander of the Empire, Order of the Emerald. Some were honourary titles, given in other countries to earlier kings. On the news last night they recited all the titles. My head was swimming!"

"Maybe . . . ." Pausing, Sarah looked out to sea. "Duncan, there's the yacht!" As a flare lit the night, the sea turned crimson. In the bright light, they saw a powerful yacht. It was white, with a sleek arrangement of upper decks.

As the cousins stared, the yacht came closer. Then, on its bridge, a signal light began to flash.

Quickly Tom pulled out his notebook. Liz and Sarah called out the signal letters while Duncan studied the yacht through his spyglass. "W," Liz called, "I...L...L...R...E...C...E...I...V...E . . . " When the message was over, Sarah repeated it. *"Will receive Ice Diamond 2230-11-23."*

"That means 10:30 p.m. on November 23," Tom said, looking at his pocket calendar, "and that's soon! What *is* the Ice Diamond? And where's the hiding place? It must be around here, because the signal's flashing at the Harbour. Who else can see it?"

"The yacht's leaving," Sarah said. The flare's red glow had died away, but the big boat's running lights were visible as it plunged away through the Atlantic waves. "Is that the same yacht from last time, Duncan?"

He nodded. "We've got to really move on finding the Ice Diamond! It's not long until November 23 and we don't even know if it's a jewel. It could be anything, maybe a smuggler's code."

"Hey, guys," Liz said in excitement. She was looking through the spyglass at the village far below. "Something's happening at the church."

The others came to her side. "What is it?" Tom asked.

"Try the spyglass," Liz said, handing it to him.

The church leapt into focus. The powerful spyglass even showed small details, like the old tombstones leaning in the church yard. Two figures in black were at the church door, going inside. Parked nearby was the Jeep with RENEGADE on it.

"Remember we told you about the Renegades?" Tom said to his cousins. "Well, they've reached Petty Harbour already. They're after the church records, to find out where Old Man Livingstone was born. We've got to warn the police."

"We can phone from our house," Duncan said, as they began running down the hill. "But the police station is in Mount Pearl, so they'll be a while getting here."

At the house the boys rushed inside to phone. Liz and Sarah continued down the hill, running past the cozy houses where TV screens glowed and people laughed together. The streets were deserted.

Liz held up a hand as they reached the main road. Close by was the church. It was tall and stood on a hill. Nearby were the tombstones, dark and crooked.

Parked in the shadow of the church was the Jeep. Something glowed inside it. "That's probably a cellular phone," Liz said. "The Renegades must be inside the church, searching for the birth records. If they can find where Richard's grandfather was born, they'll know where the Ice Diamond is hidden."

Together the cousins ran from tombstone to tombstone, watching for movement at the church. Cautiously they slipped in the open door, studying the darkness. The church smelled of flowers and hymn books, but they couldn't see anything. Then a flashlight beam cut the darkness.

"That looks like the church office they're in," Liz whispered.

In the flashlight's glow they saw the Renegades leaning over a desk. On it was a thick book. The couple whispered together, then suddenly the man slammed the book with his fist. "Nothing in here, either! Maybe these are the wrong books. All we've seen are records about marriages. Nothing on births."

"We'll keep looking."

"I'm really starting to hate this job," the man said. "I told you old churches make me nervous, and here we are inside one. Let's get out of here."

"One last look," his partner said. She reached for another leather-bound book, and began turning the pages. "These books are incredibly dusty. My asthma's bothering me something . . . ."

"Hey," the man exclaimed. "I just heard a noise!"

Liz and Sarah ducked behind a pew, and watched a flashlight beam crawl around the church walls. "It was probably a mouse," the woman said. "You're just on edge. Give me a few more minutes, I'm sure we can find those birth records."

"I don't like this." The man's voice was a low growl. "You know how I feel about going back to prison. It's so lonely behind those walls. We almost got captured by those kids at the mansion. If the boss hadn't untied us, we'd have been in a prison cell right now."

"Forget it. Those kids got lucky once, only. Now shut up, I'm trying to concentrate. Soon as we find out where the old guy was born, we'll know the hiding place. Then we'll move in, grab the Ice Diamond for the boss, and collect our money. We'll fly home first class."

"You promise?"

"For sure."

"Hey — over there. Look!"

"What is it now?" the woman said angrily. "Another mouse?"

"No! Out the window. *Look!*"

In the churchyard two figures had risen from behind tombstones. One wore a dark overcoat and a cloth cap. His face was twisted, the nose bent sideways and the mouth crooked. The second figure was small, with a face that was also bent out of shape. Her hair resembled a white mop, and she leaned on a cane.

As the figures began moving toward the church, there was a scream from the office. Then the man ran, crashing past the pews and out the open door. Seconds later the Jeep roared into life. Cursing, the woman ran outside. Liz and Sarah raced to the window in time to see the Renegades tearing away in the Jeep, then they looked at the figures in the churchyard. One pulled the mop off, then tossed away the dress to reveal a boy in jeans and ski jacket. Next to go was the nylon which had squeezed his face out of shape.

"Duncan!" Sarah laughed. "I knew it was you guys."

Tom pulled off his disguise. "This is mummering gear, Liz! People in Newfoundland wear these disguises to visit their friends. We threw on the clothes after we phoned the police. I remembered churches make that guy nervous, so we wanted to scare them away from the birth records."

Duncan was bouncing around with excitement. "That was so great, the way he ran! I couldn't believe my eyes."

"Did it work?" Tom asked his sister. "Or did they find something?"

Liz shook her head. "No, but maybe we can find where Richard's grandfather was born."

Inside the church office they flicked a switch, and warm light glowed over the desk. "Here's some more books," Liz said, pointing to a shelf over the door. Standing on a chair, she studied them. "These are the birth records! I'm glad the Renegades didn't notice this shelf." Taking down a volume marked L-M-N she carried it to the desk. "What we need could easily be in here." Quickly Liz leafed through the thick old book, then gasped in surprise.

"It's gone! Someone's ripped out the page."

"Who did it?" Duncan said. "The Renegades?"

Liz shook her head. "They didn't open this book. Someone got here before the Renegades."

"You mean tonight?" Sarah said. "But how do you know? The page could have been ripped out years ago."

Liz stood on the chair and lifted down another book. "Open this one." Thick dust rose to their faces, making them cough. "It hasn't been touched in a long time," she said, "but the volume we used wasn't dusty, so it's been opened recently. Someone got here shortly before the Renegades and stole that page. I wonder who?"

*   *   *

Early the next morning they were interviewed about the break-in by two police officers. Afterwards, the cousins discussed the case over a big breakfast of bacon and eggs with pancakes and maple syrup.

"We're running out of time," Tom said, looking at a chart showing suspects and motives, and the hours remaining until 22:30 on November 23. "Where else could we search? Up along the cliffs? Is there an abandoned lighthouse, or something like that?"

Duncan sat straight up. "Yes! I never thought of that. You've done it, Tom!"

"Done what?"

"Figured out where to search! Down the coast is a lighthouse with an abandoned place beside it. The keeper lived there until the light was automated. Now the house is deserted — it's the perfect hiding place."

"How do we get there?"

"Boat is fastest, but Dad's working on ours this morning." Duncan thought for a minute. "Ginger Watson! She drives south every weekend to visit relatives. She'll be leaving in an hour, so let's get a lift. It's an easy walk from the highway to the lighthouse."

Upstairs, they were pulling on winter clothes when Mrs. Austen appeared with Liz and Sarah. "We're going for a walk," she said. "I'd like you to come along. There's something I want to tell you."

"Sure, Mom," Tom said.

Soon they were walking downhill past white and green and orange houses. Pale sunlight cast shadows behind a picket fence, where a tabby cat enjoyed its morning bath. Strong winds blew in from the Atlantic, bringing a pleasing smell.

"I wrote a letter to Michelle last night," Tom told his sister. "You know, the girl I met in Québec. I told her this place is beautiful. Maybe some day she'll see it with me."

Liz nodded. "The Harbour's wonderful."

At the various docks and stages, people were working on their boats. They talked to each other across the misty water, discussing the break-in. Beyond them, the church stood on a hill. The spire was very tall.

Reaching the waterfront road, they followed it in the direction of the church. Mrs. Austen paused outside a house with a big clothesline. "When I was 18, I was going to marry a boy named Harold and live in this house. I'd probably have been there still, washing clothes and sweeping the floor. But you know what happened? An argument about hockey changed my life."

"What happened Mom?" Tom asked.

"You see those men talking at the end of the road, near the church? That corner's called The Stand. The retired men hang out there, telling stories about the old days."

Mrs. Austen paused.

"For generations this village was divided by people's beliefs. There were constant arguments between people who lived on the north side of the water and those who lived south. Both groups had hockey teams, but neither won much."

"One day some men were at The Stand, arguing about which team was best. Mom and I happened to be passing, and she blew her top. She said they were crazy not to have one united team. In those days women weren't supposed to have opinions, so the men told her to take a hike. But Nanny stuck to her idea, and others started agreeing with her."

Mrs. Austen's face glowed. "What courage! Back then women were supposed to obey orders and keep quiet, so their husbands and fathers weren't happy at all."

"What happened to the teams?" Tom asked.

"Eventually they were combined. Since then the Harbour's produced some real champions."

Mrs. Austen looked at the house with the big clothesline. "I wanted to do something with my life, but I was under a lot of pressure to marry Harold. Then Nanny told me things were changing for women, and I had a part to play. I decided I could be courageous too, so I cancelled my wedding and left for Winnipeg to attend university. I became a lawyer, married your Dad and started to make my dreams come true."

She looked at the four cousins. "I just want you to know that story. I'm proud of Nanny and all the women who set an example for the rest of us."

She looked at her watch. "Time to get home. Thanks for listening."

"Thanks for telling us," Liz said. She and Sarah said goodbye to the boys, and left with Mrs. Austen. Duncan glanced at his watch, then gasped. "We're late! We're supposed to be going to the lighthouse with Ginger Watson. But look at the time — she may have left already!"

8

Beyond the harbour, the cold wind drove waves high against the cliffs. Grey seas surged against the breakwater, but in its shelter, the schooner was safe.

Richard Livingstone was on deck checking the canvas when Tom and Duncan raced past. "What's the big hurry?" he called. "You in training for the Olympics?"

Stopping, Tom sucked air into his lungs. "We're . . . we're late for a ride."

"Who with? Anyone I know?"

A nearby door opened, and Ginger Watson came out. Her face was red with anger as she stared at Richard. "You lied to everyone," she shouted. "There was a bulletin on the news! The Livingstone Villas project has been cancelled. The tenants you're kicking out won't have anywhere to live."

Richard tried to ignore Ginger, but she marched across the rocky land to the breakwater. "What will happen now to the tenants? Will you cancel the park and let them keep their homes? Please don't tear down those buildings!"

Richard glanced at her. "A contract's a contract. They must be out November 30." He sighed. "But I'm sorry the Villas fell through — it was a beautiful dream."

Ginger went inside and slammed the door, making the wall shake. Duncan and Tom timidly approached the house, and knocked. The door flew open.

"What?" Ginger yelled.

"Um . . . ." Tom said. "We were, uh, wondering . . . ."

"Wondering what?"

With a bright smile, Duncan asked for a ride south. Ginger nodded, gave the schooner an angry look, then motioned at a small garage. "The car's in there. Wait for me."

Soon they were on the road in a red Tercel, climbing the hill out of town. "There's no public demand for the park," Ginger grumbled. "There's already another park two blocks away. It's just to satisfy that man's pride. The newspaper in St. John's did a survey, and ninety percent of the people wanted the tenants to keep their homes." The car crossed a bridge, then drove past a pretty lake framed by trees with bare branches. "When I look out my window and see that schooner, I feel like weeping. I keep hoping someone will steal it and sink the thing at sea."

Reaching the Goulds, Duncan asked to stop at a general store. Inside, they explored the racks and made their purchases, then returned to the car. The wind and sky were different.

"Fog's coming," Duncan said.

"The weather changes fast around here!"

"It's never boring, that's for sure."

As they got in beside Ginger, a car came off the highway and stopped. It was the Citroen with the mud-splattered body. Tom stared at the driver.

"He's the Hawk! The guy from the barber shop."

"What a handsome man," Ginger said. "Care to introduce me?"

As she reversed out of the parking lot, Tom grabbed Duncan's arm. "Duck! He's looking this way." They stayed low until they were on the highway and heading south, then sat up.

"Any sign of being followed?" Tom asked Ginger.

She glanced in the rearview mirror. "Nope."

Tom looked down a side road. "Hey, there's the Renegades!" He watched the Jeep until it disappeared from sight. "It was parked beside a BMW with tinted windows. I couldn't see who was inside."

"I bet they were meeting with their boss," Duncan said. "Did you see the personalized plate on the BMW? It said POWER. That's a strange choice."

"Maybe it's an acronym. P could stand for Planned, maybe O for Operations, um . . . maybe . . . ."

"Wait," Duncan said. "I've got it!" He scribbled in his notebook. "It means Plunder Only With Experienced Robbers."

"Could be," Tom laughed, "or maybe it doesn't mean anything."

Ginger smiled. "You've got a good mind, Duncan. No wonder you found my car keys so fast."

"That case was too simple, but at least it earned my agency its first loonie."

Tom looked at Ginger. "Do the words Ice Diamond mean anything to you?"

"Nope," she said, yawning. "Duncan already asked me that."

They passed through a long stretch of forested country before seeing the open Atlantic again. Highway signs warned of moose, and occasionally they went through villages of scattered houses and wooden buildings that advertised gasoline and videos.

Ginger glanced at Tom. "Did Richard Livingstone ever mention his son?"

Tom nodded.

"He doesn't share his father's twisted values. He moved to Toronto, and went into business there. People say he's been very successful in an incredibly short time."

The car stopped beside the highway, and the boys jumped out. They waved as Ginger pulled away in her Tercel. "Meet me here at exactly five p.m.," she called. "I'm not waiting if you're late!"

Duncan smiled. "Ginger doesn't mean that. She's got a kind heart."

They began walking along a lonely, rutted road between thin trees. Cold, wet mist touched their faces as fog rolled in from sea. "Hey, this is something!" Tom knelt beside an old, rusty cannon abandoned beside the road. "See these initials? *G.R. That means George Rex!*"

"He was a king long ago, right?"

Tom nodded. "Which means this cannon was actually in the War of 1812. I can't believe my eyes. It's not in a museum, it's *here,* lying by this road."

They both stared at the cannon. Tom took a picture, and they moved on. Jumping over large puddles, sometimes slipping on mud, they followed the road out the empty headland. Fog blew past them, wheeling and rolling, its grey mists hiding the sea.

Finally they reached the lonely lighthouse. Its beam

swept the fog and a horn bellowed. The windows of the keeper's abandoned house were smashed and empty, and the ground was littered with junk. "Lonely place," Tom said.

"Sorry we came?"

"Nope, but I keep wishing my Dad was here. He'd know what to do."

"He'll arrive soon," Duncan said. "Meanwhile let's gather him some background information."

Tom looked up at the empty windows of the abandoned house. Something moved inside, probably a strip of wallpaper blowing in the wind. "Actually, this would be a perfect hiding place for a jewel. Who'd want to go in there?"

As they walked closer, Tom pointed at the muddy ground beside a shack. "Look at those tire tracks, Duncan. They're recent — the treads are really clear!" He studied the ground. "There's a puddle of oil. In the parkade in St. John's, that muddy Citroen was dripping oil. I remember seeing it while the Hawk and Richard talked inside the car."

Tom looked at the nearby house. "I bet the Hawk parks the Citroen here, then goes inside."

"You're probably right," Duncan said. "But why?"

"I don't know," Tom said. "But we're going to find out."

*　　　*　　　*

Inside the house the wind moaned through the empty windows, and bare wires flapped against the walls. Layers of old wallpaper hung in shreds.

"Wicked place," Duncan whispered. "It's so cold in here."

"No signs of recent use. Let's check the upper floor."

"I just heard something — maybe a car coming!"

Tom went quickly to a window. There was nothing to see but thick fog pressing close. "Let's take a quick look upstairs, then get out of here."

The upper rooms looked pathetic with their broken windows and floors that were littered with rubbish soaked by many rains. "No clues here," Tom said. He picked up a soggy book. "An illustrated history of Edinburgh Castle." Water dripped as he turned it over. "Dietmar Oban has some roots in Scotland. I'll take this home for him."

"Gross," Duncan said.

Just then a footstep sounded below. Looking down the stairs, Tom saw the Hawk come in the door from outside.

As the man brushed moisture off his dark winter coat, Tom and Duncan pressed against the wall, trying not to breathe. The Hawk moved out of sight. His footsteps sounded clearly below, followed by the creak of hinges. Seconds later there was a soft thump, then silence. Outside the abandoned house, a seagull screamed.

Tom and Duncan crept down the staircase. Through a broken window, they saw the muddy Citroen parked outside.

In a dark corner of the room, Tom spotted a trap door with rusty hinges. Hurrying forward with Duncan, he lifted it. Cold air rose into their faces. "There's some stairs cut into the rock," Tom whispered. "Let's see where they go."

Switching on the flashlights they'd brought along, Tom and Duncan started down the stairs. The twin beams danced around the stone walls. "It's an old mine," Tom whispered, as they reached the bottom of the rock stairs. "That's a tunnel ahead."

A rough path led forward to a widening in the rocky mine. "I can smell the ocean," Duncan said. "See where those rocks have come down? We could probably climb over them, and get out to the Atlantic."

"There's the remains of an old dock," Tom said, pointing. "That's how the ore was taken out to sea. Richard Livingstone had a picture of this mine at his mansion. His grandfather owned it."

"That guy turns up everywhere," Duncan said. His words echoed with a hollow sound. "Why the rock stairs under the lighthouse? A secret escape route?"

Tom nodded. "Could be. Maybe it was for the miners to escape, in case of some disaster underground."

The boys moved deeper into the mine. Water dripped, and the air grew thick with moisture. Their flashlights made shadows on the rocky walls. As the mine narrowed, creatures were heard scuttling away.

Tom's heart was beating fast. "I think . . . ."

Suddenly Duncan grabbed his arm. "Look!"

Tom's flashlight swept the darkness, then its beam found a small pile of rocks straight ahead. Resting on the rocks was a skull.

Next to the skull was an old piece of wood. Carved into it was a grim warning. STAY AWAY the sign said. DANGER HERE.

Duncan studied the skull. "It's not human. It's a deer, or some animal like that." He examined the sign. "This was made recently. See where the letters were carved — the wood's still white. The cuts haven't aged yet."

Tom's flashlight beam travelled along the rocky mine. It was narrow and very dark. "No sign of the Hawk. Want to turn back?"

There was silence, then Duncan said, "No."

"Neither do I."

They moved forward. Tom swallowed — his mouth was dry. "What's that ahead? It looks like a wooden tunnel, built inside the walls of the mine."

Tom and Duncan stepped into the wooden tunnel. Their footsteps echoed as they walked through it, then again they were surrounded by the rock walls of the mine. "Look at this," Tom said, stopping beside a stainless steel panel attached to the rock. On it were two switches, but nothing happened when Tom tried them. "They probably need to be activated by a key."

"What do the switches control?" Duncan asked.

"Maybe something about that wooden tunnel."

Their flashlights found stairs cut into the mine's rocky wall. "More stairs! They lead up. I wonder where they go?"

With their hands on the rocky wall, Tom and Duncan climbed the rough stairs until they finally ended. Tom found a door handle, but it wouldn't open. He leaned his ear against the door, listening to low sounds behind it.

"Voices?" he whispered to Duncan. "I can't tell for sure."

His cousin concentrated on the sounds, then shook his head. "It could be anything."

"What'll we do now?"

Duncan shone his flashlight on his watch. "We're almost late for meeting Ginger. We'd better get moving."

"Okay," Tom said. They hurried down the stairs into the mine. "What'll we do next?"

"I'm not sure. Any ideas?"

"The funeral's tomorrow, so let's wait until it's over, then tell people what we've found."

"Good idea," Duncan said. "Besides, your Dad's due in town tomorrow. He can help us."

"There's that strange wooden tunnel ahead." Tom's

flashlight picked out the switches on the stainless steel panel. "I still can't figure what those are for," he said. "But somehow they give me the creeps."

*   *   *

They met Ginger safely, and she soon dropped them off in Petty Harbour. Tom looked at the old men gathered at the Stand. "Would they tell me a sea story?"

"Probably," Duncan replied. "Let's go ask."

An old man smiled at their request. "I'll tell you about the *Despatch*." His face was deeply lined, and his blue eyes were kind. "Looking at you," he said to Tom, "I can tell you love animals. This story's about a Newfoundland dog. You know the kind — they're big and strong, and can handle winter storms."

Another man came closer. "You telling the *Despatch* story again, Raymond?" He looked at the boys. "It's a true story, you know."

The first man nodded. "A brig called the *Despatch* piled into a reef in a fierce Atlantic storm. People were trapped on board, seeing land close by, but unable to swim the raging seas. Well, do you know, a Newfoundland dog swam those waves to the *Despatch,* took a rope in its teeth and fought its way to shore, where its master waited. That lifeline was the reason those people reached safety."

The other man pointed at a nearby house. "History Fred lives there. He just returned to town from a research trip. Go ask him for stories, he's got a million."

"Great," Tom said. "Thanks for that one. It was cool."

They knocked on the door of the small house. A floorboard creaked inside the door, then it was opened by a man about 30. His sweater was rumpled, and cat fur clung to his trousers. "Yes?" he asked, removing his half-moon glasses.

"Hi, History Fred," Duncan said. "This is my cousin, Tom Austen. He's from Winnipeg."

"Here for the funeral, I suppose." History Fred waved them inside. "I liked your grandmother. I collected many of her greatest stories." In the small kitchen he filled bowls with food for three cats who anxiously watched from the floor, and then poured tea from a cracked Brown Betty teapot. "Help yourself to something from the fridge. What can I do you for?"

"I'd love to hear some stories," Tom said. "The men at the Stand said you've got a million."

History Fred smiled. "I've never counted." He led them into the next room, where banks of video equipment lined the walls. As the man flicked switches he gestured at a nearby shelf lined with videos. "Pick any subject, and I've got an interview with someone about it."

"Got anything about an Ice Diamond?" Tom asked. "It may be a jewel, or possibly a code word."

History Fred turned to a computer and worked quickly. Then he said, "Find a video with the label GX-435. My index says it mentions an Ice Diamond."

"Hey, we're getting somewhere!" Tom grinned at Duncan. "Lucky we came over."

Within seconds a screen glowed, and a woman was seen. Her hair was white, and she wore thick glasses. The image bounced as History Fred hit fast forward, then stopped.

"This is Mrs. Lucy Chalmers," he said. "I interviewed her six months ago. There was a technical problem, so I lost most of the interview. Only this part remains."

The image stopped bouncing, and Mrs. Chalmers spoke. "I remember once, when I was young, a sailing ship entered our harbour. On board was a king from a distant land. He stayed with Old Man Livingstone, at his cabin, and visited with us each day. The king was sailing the world, seeking to learn about people and speak of peace — a wonderful man. My parents were deeply moved, and led a movement to create a special award for the king. It was presented at the community hall. Everyone was there."

History Fred's voice spoke from off camera. "What did the award look like?"

"It was a painting done by a local lady. It showed sunbeams reflecting from the ice at sea. Under the picture the words read, *Let us cherish our world.*"

"Was there a name for the award?"

Mrs. Chalmers nodded. "It was called the Order of the Ice Diamond. I guess because of how the sunlight reflects from the ice. Anyway, the King was thrilled. Later he died, and the Order of the Ice Diamond passed to his son. There was another son, I think, but I lost track. I think the final king was killed in a revolution."

"Can you tell me more about . . . ."

The screen went blank. "That's when the equipment broke down," said History Fred. "Really annoying. I've tried to interview Mrs. Chalmers again, but she's usually in Labrador with her children's families. I love the stories these seniors tell!" He aimed the remote control at the video terminal and the screen went blank. "Mrs. Chalmers is coming back for the funeral tomorrow. If you want to know more, you could ask her then."

"Perfect," Duncan said. "We'll question her the moment the funeral's over."

"Got any videos on Richard Livingstone's son?" Tom asked History Fred.

"Sure, lots. Anything in particular?"

"When he left for Toronto."

"Coming up."

History Fred grabbed a video, and soon a young man appeared on the screen. He had Richard's blond hair and handsome eyes, but he looked sad. Reporters and cameras and microphones were jammed around him. "I can't watch my father operate any more," said the young man. "He has no respect for people, or for the world we share. I'm going to Toronto. I owe myself a fresh start."

A microphone was shoved closer to his face. "You'll never return?" the reporter demanded.

"Perhaps one day."

When the video ended, the boys thanked History Fred and left the house. Evening was coming. The sea air smelled good, and a light breeze touched their faces. Waves slapped lightly against the breakwater. "I'd love a trip in your family's boat. Are we allowed to use it?"

"Sure," Duncan said. "Dad and Mom taught me the controls."

"How about a trip down the coast?"

"Where to?"

Tom shrugged. "How about getting a look at the lighthouse from the sea? Maybe we can spot the entrance to that old mine."

"Hey!" Duncan grinned. "What a great idea."

*   *   *

The dark seas ran high as the little boat carried Tom and Duncan south. Then they saw the lighthouse above on the cliff, and beside it the abandoned house where the keeper used to live.

"Say," Tom said, "I recognize this scene from a picture at Richard's mansion. Same lighthouse and cliffs, and the same cove."

Duncan studied the coast with his spyglass. "I can see a narrow opening in the cliffs. That's probably the old entrance to the mine." He turned, and looked further south. "Hey!"

"What is it?"

Duncan handed him the spyglass. In Tom's magnified vision foam blew off distant waves, then a Zodiac crested a wave. The black rubber boat was coming their way, moving fast.

Inside were four figures in wet suits. "I bet those are the guys Liz and I saw at the airport. They had a Zodiac and tents. They must be camping out in the wilderness somewhere. Could they be hunters?"

"Maybe," Duncan said, "but it's getting dark. What are they hunting?"

Tom watched the Zodiac turn toward the cove and run ashore on a small rocky beach. "They're getting out, and studying a map. One guy's pointing up the cliff. Here — use your spyglass."

Duncan studied the scene with the spyglass. Then at last he said, "They're leaving in the Zodiac, heading south. They must have only come to check out the cove. Want to follow them?"

Tom shook his head. "That Zodiac's too fast compared to your boat. Let's head home."

"Any theories about those guys?" Duncan asked, turning the wheel into the wind.

"A voice inside me whispers bounty hunters. They've been paid to come to Newfoundland and capture something or someone."

"Who?"

"I've no idea."

"And you figure the Renegades are also bounty hunters?"

"Yes, but probably working for a different boss." Tom shielded his face against the raw wind. "The question is, who do the Renegades work for? And who's the boss of those guys in the Zodiac?"

* * *

The next morning the sky was grey. "Bad weather coming," Duncan said, looking out the window. In the house everyone was in black for the funeral. People cried, and comforted each other with hugs.

The cemetery was on a hill, high above the village. Mist clung to the cliffs that loomed above the houses clustered around the harbour. Many people had climbed the hill to be with Nanny's family.

The wind blew through the wild grass surrounding older graves. A tombstone dated 1850 lay on its back; near it, names and dates had vanished from a weathered wooden cross. Further up the hill, boulders had been scattered by a glacier retreating many lifetimes before.

Nanny's grave was beside her husband, who had died two years earlier. Following the religious ceremony, the priest turned to Duncan and Sarah's mother.

"Will you remember your mother for us, Lesley?"

"Yes." She was a tall woman, with long red hair and a lightly-freckled nose. In her arms was the family's new baby, Samantha. "I . . . . " She paused, struggling to control her emotions. "I . . . . "

"Aunt Lesley's taking it hard," Liz whispered to Tom.

Their aunt wiped her eyes with a damp hankie. "I . . . Well, I can only say one thing. Life's going to be hard without my Mom around. That's for sure." Tears rolled from her eyes. "But in my arms I hold a future friend." She kissed the baby's forehead, then looked at the cousins. "Samantha is lucky. She'll grow up in tomorrow's world. Caring kids like you will be adults before long, and running things. You'll be strong leaders, and people will be peaceful and happy."

She turned to her husband, and he hugged her. The priest looked at Mrs. Austen, and she stepped forward. She wore a black coat and hat that made her red hair more vivid.

Mrs. Austen squeezed Aunt Lesley's hand, then looked at the solemn faces of the people around the grave. "Mom taught me a lot," she said. "Even at the hospital in St. John's, I was still learning from her. She looked at me with those Irish eyes, and told me how she finally understood the patterns of her life. The pain and the laughter, the good times and the bad, they all made sense at last. As she lay dying, Mom finally understood exactly what her life had been for. She was so peaceful at the end."

Mrs. Austen turned to her other sister. "Now you, Melody."

Aunt Melody's hair and eyes were black and very beautiful. Liz leaned close to Sarah. "Isn't she wonderful? She's such a famous opera singer that she's even been interviewed on some major TV show in Paris."

"I saw her on *Entertainment Tonight* during the summer," Sarah whispered.

"Me too!"

Aunt Melody looked at the mourners. The wind touched her hair. "I learned of my mother's illness while visiting friends in a villa overlooking the Mediterranean Sea. We were surrounded by sunny white walls and flowers. We'd been discussing what Canada means to people in other countries. Know what my friends said? All over the world, people love the idea of Canada and countries like ours. Places of real freedom, where people are happy despite their problems. Countries where there's always a helping hand for others."

She paused. "My mother taught me strength. She said to always speak out about your beliefs. Today, in her memory, I speak out for Canada. Let this country live and be united, for ourselves and for people everywhere."

Aunt Melody studied the watching faces. "If we believe in Canada, let's start saying so. With strong, clear voices."

Several people nodded, then the priest smiled. "Thank you," he said to the sisters. "You spoke beautifully."

For a while people stayed in the cemetery, talking, then began the walk down to the family home. "See that lady with the thick glasses?" Tom said to Liz. "That's Mrs. Chalmers. We're going to ask her some questions."

"I wish Dad's flight hadn't been delayed by fog," Liz said. "Now he won't arrive until tomorrow." She looked at Kathy Munro, who was walking down the hill beside her secretary, Dave Foster. Richard Livingstone was further behind, talking to the priest but watching Kathy.

Sarah moved closer to Mrs. Austen. "I liked what you said at the cemetery, Auntie."

"Thanks, Sarah. You know, I'm glad you cousins are friends. You'll do lots together in life. That's wonderful." Mrs. Austen smiled, but tears rose in her eyes. "I'm so emotional today. I need a cup of tea and strong arms. Liz, I'm so glad your Dad's arriving tomorrow."

*　　　*　　　*

At the house, they looked down the hill. Restless waves tossed against the breakwater, and storm clouds were gathering over the Atlantic. As evening approached the wind grew stronger, tossing white water higher and higher against the darkening cliffs.

"This'll be a major storm," Duncan said.

Richard paused on the porch steps beside Mrs.

Chalmers. They chatted until Kathy Munro and Dave Foster arrived at the house with Mrs. Austen. Richard held up a hand to stop her. "We haven't met," he said, and introduced himself. "I'm going to marry Kathy."

Dave Foster went inside the house. As he did, Mrs. Austen said, "I just met Kathy, and she mentioned your engagement. Congratulations."

Richard nodded briefly. "I'm hoping for a happier wedding day than my friend Harold. He was left waiting at the altar, right here in Petty Harbour. I met him years later in the city, and he told me about it. What a bitter, unhappy man."

Mrs. Austen's piercing blue eyes looked at him. "Sure, and you know why? Because he couldn't find a wife prepared to be his servant. He wanted someone to wash his socks and sew his buttons. Not me, thanks."

"So!" Richard stepped closer to her. "Then you admit it! You *are* the one who abandoned Harold on his wedding day."

Mrs. Austen smiled. "I hope my mother's listening to this conversation from above, Mr. Livingstone. I remember her talking to me about Harold when I was seventeen. He was so good looking, and I was blinded by starlight. Then one day I stopped dreaming about wearing a lacy dress up the aisle, and I pictured Harold as a husband and father. He was already ordering me around, and we weren't even married. Besides, he wasn't fair and he wasn't kind. I finally got smart. I admit, it was at the last minute. But I've never regretted my decision."

Richard snorted. "You broke your promise to Harold. Decent people honour promises."

"Indeed?" Mrs. Austen studied him. "I believe you made a promise to your tenants in St. John's. Something about providing new accomodation?" She opened the front door, then looked at Richard a final time.

"Interesting to have met you, Mr. Livingstone."

She went inside with Ginger, who had listened to it all and was grinning happily. Richard made an angry noise, then also went into the house. Duncan turned to Mrs. Chalmers. "May we ask you something, Mrs. Chalmers? We saw you on a video, talking about the Order of the Ice Diamond. Lately there's been a yacht signalling from offshore about an Ice Diamond. Do you see any connection?"

"Recently," Mrs. Chalmers replied, "I read a magazine article about a Prince who's in hiding. I'm sure it was his ancestor who visited Petty Harbour when I was a child. The king was honoured with the Order of the Ice Diamond, and that title was passed down from generation to generation."

Duncan's eyes glowed with excitement. "I think I see a connection!"

Mrs. Chalmers turned to the others. "The Ice Diamond may be the Prince. He could be in hiding somewhere near Petty Harbour."

Liz and Tom stared at each other. "Of course," Liz exclaimed. "Ice Diamond is a code word for that Prince. It's not a jewel at all. The Prince turns 18 at midnight! *The yacht's coming for him!*"

"Maybe they're friends, come to take the Prince home," Sarah suggested.

Liz shook her head. "Then why hide out at sea, instead of coming into port? No, I bet revolutionaries are on that yacht. They're afraid of losing control of their country. Those bounty hunters are trying to find the Prince so he can be sold to the revolutionaries. Then the Prince will be dropped overboard from the yacht to drown. He's got to be warned."

"But where can he be hiding?" Duncan said.

Tom turned to Mrs. Chalmers. "Would you happen to

know where Richard Livingstone's grandfather was
born?"

"Certainly," she replied. "South of here, not far from
the lighthouse. He was born in a log cabin. The last I
heard, the cabin was still standing. It was solidly built,
with a big fireplace."

"Of course!" Tom said. "I remember seeing a picture
of the mine at Richard's mansion. It showed a cabin on
the cliff, hidden back in the trees." He turned to Duncan.
"Remember we discovered that secret route from the
lighthouse? It led through the mine to the place where I
thought we heard voices. That could easily have been the
Prince talking to his bodyguard. They're in the cabin,
which is linked to the lighthouse by the route through the
mine." He turned to Liz and Sarah. "And you know who
the bodyguard is? *The Hawk.*"

9

As Mrs. Chalmers went inside, Tom looked at his watch.
"We've got to warn the Prince. Duncan and Sarah, can
we use your boat?"

"Of course!"

Together they raced down the hill toward the harbour.
A few cozy lights shone from houses, but the wind
outside was cold. Reaching the main road, they heard the
roar of a powerful engine. "The Renegades," Tom yelled.
"I know that sound! Into hiding, quick!"

The cousins scrambled behind a fence and dropped to
the ground as the Jeep sped out of the darkness. It skid-
ded to a stop beside a pay phone, and the woman jumped
out. She consulted a piece of paper, then punched num-

bers on the phone and began talking. Her voice was loud, carried by the wind. "I couldn't hear you on the cellular phone. Too much static. That's why I'm phoning back from here. Now, where'd you say the Ice Diamond is hiding? How do we find him? A secret tunnel from what lighthouse?"

Tom and Liz exchanged a glance. "The Renegades get their information fast," Tom whispered moments later as the Jeep raced away. "I bet they're heading for the light-house."

"Look, that woman forgot her piece of paper. It'll show the number she just called."

The cousins ran forward. "I don't believe it," Sarah said, looking at the number. She turned to Duncan with enormous eyes. "It's *our* phone number!"

*　　　*　　　*

At the boat, Duncan and Sarah quickly threw off the lines. "Why our phone number?" Duncan demanded. "Is someone there feeding inside information to the Renegades?" He turned to Tom. "Why do you think the Hawk kept warning you away?"

"He was super paranoid, so he was probably afraid I'd tell the media about the Prince hiding in Newfoundland. If reporters located the Prince, the bounty hunters could have grabbed him. No wonder the Hawk was upset when he heard me talking at the barber shop about an Ice Diamond."

Leaving the breakwater they saw Richard Livingstone alone on the deck of his schooner, scanning the night with binoculars. Heavy seas pounded the cliffs as the boat headed south with Sarah at the helm. For a while, nobody spoke. Then Tom said, "I still can't believe it. The Ice Diamond was never a jewel, it was a code. I'd been picturing a perfect diamond flashing with colour. I couldn't wait to see it."

"You know what I can't believe?" Liz said. "Our mother actually left a man standing at the altar. What romance!" She shielded her face against the gusting wind. "Is that the lighthouse ahead?"

Tom nodded. "There's the keeper's abandoned place, beside the lighthouse." He used Duncan's spyglass to study the cliff. "The cabin isn't visible from sea level."

Sarah slowed the boat as they approached the cove. Waves roared up against the rock, but a small harbour sheltered the old entrance to the mine. Over the years rocks had crashed down across the entrance, but a section of dock remained.

They scrambled over the rocks and were soon inside the mine, following the beams of their flashlights under rock ceilings that dripped with water. As the cousins whispered to each other, their voices echoed inside the narrow mine.

Then Liz screamed. "A skull! Straight ahead, a skull!"

"It's okay," Tom said. "That's not human, it's a deer's skull. It's just a defence, like that sign."

"A defence against what?"

"Probably snoops like us." Tom's flashlight found the wooden tunnel ahead. "See that stainless-steel panel?" His words echoed as they passed through the tunnel. "I'm sure those switches control the tunnel in some way."

Beyond the tunnel they reached the stairs cut into the rock. "Do these lead to the lighthouse?" Sarah whispered.

"No," Tom said. He started up the stairs. "These go to the Prince's hiding place." Climbing, they were surrounded by darkness, except for a sliver of light from under a door. At the top of the rock stairs, Tom pounded the door with his hand.

"Please let us in," he shouted. "The Prince is in great danger!"

Moments later the door opened. Yellow candlelight shone on the fierce eyes of the Hawk. Beyond him was a cabin made of big logs. There was a stone fireplace, thick rugs on the wooden floor, and furniture made of pine and oak.

"What do you want?" the Hawk demanded. "Why have you troubled me?"

"There's danger to your Prince!"

"What prince? I've no idea . . . ."

"That Prince!" Tom exclaimed, pointing at a doorway.

Watching them was a handsome teenager. His hair and eyes were dark, and his face was strong. He wore a red-checked shirt and jeans. As he walked toward the cousins, they all stared.

They'd never seen royalty before.

*　　　*　　　*

"Hello," the Prince said, shaking hands with each of them. "You have caused great worry for my Emissary." He glanced at the Hawk. "I understand he tried to scare you boys away. I see he has failed."

Tom quickly described the Renegades. "I think they're working for someone, your Highness. Their boss wants to sell you to the revolutionaries. You're in terrible danger!"

The prince studied Tom's face. "You look honest, but I am a guest of your country. My contact person for your government has given specific instructions. We are not to leave this cabin until midnight brings my 18th birthday. Then my contact person will take me to St. John's, where I shall announce my claim to the throne of my country."

"You'll never make it!" Duncan described the signal from the yacht. "I bet some revolutionaries are on that yacht, waiting to kill you! You're the Ice Diamond, and you'll be taken out to their yacht at 22:30. You've got to hide."

"I admit the signal causes me alarm. But where can we go?"

"To Petty Harbour," Sarah said. "Our people will protect you for sure."

"Then it's decided." The prince put on a winter coat and gloves. "I arrived secretly in Newfoundland a month ago from New Zealand. I am still getting used to the cold."

"You've really lived in hiding for 15 years?" Tom asked.

The prince nodded. "I've moved secretly with my loyal servant from country to country. I can't wait to meet some girls."

Sarah was about to speak when the Emissary raised a hand. "Your Highness! Someone's in the tunnel!"

They all stared at the open door, hearing sounds come up from the mine. "It's the Renegades," Tom whispered. "They're here already."

The Emissary turned to the Prince. "Your Highness! Into hiding — immediately."

As the Prince disappeared into a nearby room, the Emissary started down the rock stairs, and the cousins followed. The man moved quickly and soon reached the tunnel. Inside the tunnel they saw the Renegades, shining flashlights on the wooden walls. "What's this thing for?" the man said.

"Some kind of trap, maybe?" The woman flashed her light on the stainless steel panel, then she suddenly saw the Emissary. "Hey, someone's in the mine!"

The man flashed his light their way. At the same

moment, the Emissary turned a key in the panel. Powerful lights flooded the mine and the wooden tunnel. The Renegades held up their arms, shielding their eyes.

"What's going on?" the man shouted.

"Surrender," the Emissary ordered.

"Forget it, pal," the man snarled. "We need that Prince, or we don't get paid. Turn him over."

"Surrender," the Emissary said again.

The man's hands became fists. With his partner beside him, he started walking forward through the wooden tunnel. "You and those kids won't stop us, pal. We've come for the Prince."

The Emissary flipped a switch. Rope nets dropped instantly from above, trapping the Renegades. They struggled, but couldn't escape the nets. "Hey," the woman shouted. "What's going on? Release us!"

"Yeah," the man yelled. "Right now!"

The Emissary reached for the second switch. From behind the walls came the sound of machinery. Then the man and woman cried out in horror.

The wooden walls of the tunnel were moving. They were closing in on the Renegades.

* * *

"Hey," the man screamed. *"Hey, stop! Turn off that switch!"*

As the Emissary watched them with unblinking eyes, Tom grabbed his arm. "Let them go," he cried. "You can't do this!" Ignoring Tom's plea, the man took a small gun from his pocket and said, "Don't think about touching that switch, young man."

"But . . . !"

The Prince came out of the darkness. "Are these the bounty hunters you feared, Emissary? You have decided to execute them?"

"Yes, your Highness."

"But you can't," Liz said angrily. "This is Canada! People don't get executed here."

"They are criminals." The Emissary watched the walls moving slowly together. As the metal of the hidden machinery squealed with a rusty sound, the Renegades shouted desperately from the nets. Tom's brain raced with possible arguments, then he saw the Prince step forward.

"This does not seem right, Emissary."

"It has always been the way of our country, your Highness. Death to those who break the law."

"Indeed?" The Prince studied his face. "Yesterday you drove to St. John's in the Citroen. You told me you were going faster than the speed limit. Death for you, as well?"

"Your highness, that is not the same."

The Prince looked at the Renegades. Their faces were frozen with fear as the walls moved in on them. Their shouts had turned to moans. "Please," the man whimpered. "Help me."

The Prince turned to his Emissary. "I order you to stop the machinery."

"Your Highness! We must follow the old traditions. Execution of criminals has always been practised by our country."

"Perhaps it's time to change." The Prince flicked the switch, and the walls stopped moving. Then slowly they began moving apart. As the Renegades cried out happily, the Prince turned to the cousins. "The Citroen is parked outside the lighthouse. We can reach Petty Harbour quickly."

"You'll be safe at the Harbour," Sarah said. "Maybe I could show you around town."

The Prince smiled. "What a nice idea. But for now, we

must hurry."

Leaving the Renegades trapped in the nets, they followed the tunnel past the skull and the warning sign. "This thing really scared us," Tom said.

"Good," the Emissary replied. "That's what I hoped for. I feared that exploring children would enter the mine and perhaps find the secret entrance to the cabin. I wanted to scare them away."

"How'd you come to Newfoundland?" Duncan asked. "Why were you hiding in that cabin?"

"The great-grandfather of my Prince once came to your land, seeking ideas on peace. He was a guest in the cabin, and always remembered the escape route through the mine to the lighthouse."

"Who built that tunnel?"

"The owner of the cabin. Around here they called him Old Man Livingstone. He was afraid of enemies, so he figured out a secret escape route through the mine to the lighthouse, and designed the wooden tunnel as a defence against attackers. I understand that Old Man Livingstone was practically a hermit, with no friends and only his grandson to raise. He did a lot of reading. He loved Edgar Allen Poe's tales of horror, so he was proud of his collapsing tunnel."

Tom looked at the Prince. "How will you get your country back? Are you going to put an army together, or something?"

"Never." The Prince raised his head proudly. "I am against violence. I will go to the World Court at the Hague. I know they will return the country to me."

Ahead they saw rocky stairs leading up. Soon they'd passed through the lighthouse keeper's abandoned house and stepped outside into the night. Above their heads, the powerful lighthouse beam swept the stormy night. The wind was much stronger, bending nearby trees and driving waves ashore far below.

"This way, your Highness," the Emissary said. "The Citroen is parked close by. We must hurry."

"That man and woman cannot escape the nets."

"I still have great fear. Two hours remain until midnight bringing your 18th birthday. Anything can happen in that time."

Then Liz pointed at the Citroen. "Hey, you've got a flat tire." Hurrying forward, she looked at the other wheels. "They're all flat! The car's been sabatoged."

"By those Renegades?" Duncan said.

"No." Liz shone her flashlight on the Jeep, which was parked nearby. Its tires were also flat. "They wouldn't have sabatoged themselves."

"Maybe . . . ." Tom paused. "I just heard something."

"What was it?" Sarah asked.

"It sounded like a twig snapping under someone's foot." Tom aimed his flashlight at the night. The beam moved slowly over rocks and trees, then stopped. "Oh no. It can't be."

Two men were watching them. Both wore black scuba gear, and both held guns.

"Give us the Prince," one man said. "Right now."

Swiftly the pair came forward. They seized the Prince and his Emissary, then looked at the cousins.

"What'll we do about them?" one said.

"Nothing, they're only kids. They can't make any difference. I'll contact the team that's covering the cabin." The man lifted a radio to his mouth. "We've got the Ice Diamond and his bodyguard. Meet us at the Zodiac, fast."

"Ten-four," a voice crackled in reply.

Moments later the men and their prisoners disappeared down a path toward the cove at the foot of the cliff. The cousins stared helplessly at each other and then Liz cried, "Come on, let's go through the mine to the boat. We've got to follow them!"

*   *   *

The boat was waiting safely at the dock as the cousins came out of the mine. Leaving the cove they were pounded by waves. "The storm's getting bad," Sarah said from the helm, "and there's no sign of the Zodiac. It's gone already."

"Let's head for the Harbour," Duncan suggested. "The Zodiac won't go to sea, it's too rough out there. They may take the Prince and his Emissary in the Zodiac to the Harbour, then transfer them into a bigger boat. That's how they'll be taken offshore to the yacht."

From the darkness came the thunder of the sea battering against the cliffs. Sarah gave the engine full throttle as their boat fought its way homeward through surging waves and howling winds. At last the lights of Petty Harbour appeared ahead. As they approached the breakwater, Duncan looked out to sea with his spyglass. "The yacht's returned! I can see it waiting offshore." He looked at his watch. "Half an hour until 22:30."

"Hey," Tom said, "I see those guys from the Zodiac! They're on board Richard Livingstone's schooner."

Four men in black crossed the deck of the *Quest* and dropped down its side to the Zodiac. Moments later the rubber boat left the shelter of the breakwater and plowed into the open sea. There was no sign of the Prince or his Emissary.

"They've got an attaché case with them," Duncan said, watching the Zodiac through his spyglass. "I bet it's full of cash. They just got paid for grabbing the Prince."

"Who's got the prisoners now?" Sarah asked.

"I don't know who's got them," Liz replied, "but I know where they are." As their little boat passed safely through the notch in the breakwater, she pointed at the schooner.

"I bet they're inside the *Quest*."

Quickly tying up the boat, the cousins agreed on a course of action. "Liz and I will get on board the schooner," Tom said. "Maybe we can free the Prince and his Emissary before the *Quest* sails. If they're taken out to that yacht, they don't have a chance."

"I'll go phone the police," Sarah said. "Duncan, you try for the Coast Guard on the marine radio in our boat. Then stand by, in case Tom and Liz need help."

*   *   *

Moments later, Tom and Liz moved through the shadowed village toward the *Quest*. The wooden houses groaned under the wind, and spray flew over the breakwater. In the darkness waves crashed ashore.

A door opened on the schooner. Scrambling out of sight, Tom and Liz watched someone in a yellow slicker struggle forward to the bow.

"I can hear the diesel engine running," Liz said. "The *Quest* is ready for sea. The Prince and his Emissary are being taken out to the yacht."

Tom nodded. "Time's running out. Let's free them."

Crouching low, they ran to the breakwater, jumped on to the schooner, and raced across the deck. Despite the breakwater's protection, the *Quest* was rocking heavily and the big wooden wheel was soaked with spray.

Liz opened the stern door. "We've got to hurry!"

Quickly they descended the narrow stairs into the cabin. The yellow light of the swaying oil lamps fell on the barrels, the stove and other shadowed places. Henry was in his cage, silently watching the Prince and his Emissary who lay on two bunks, eyes closed.

"They could be dead already," Tom said as they hurried forward.

Liz shook her head. "No, they're out cold, probably drugged."

"Can we get them up the stairs?"

"No, they're far too . . . ." Liz raised her head. "I just heard footsteps crossing the deck. We've got to hide."

Tom looked at the display of barrels. "Behind there," he said. As they slipped into hiding the door opened, and sea boots appeared. The man in the yellow slicker came down the stairs, crossed the cabin and climbed into a bucket seat. He seized the power controls, and the big diesel roared.

At the same moment, they heard the loud THUMP of feet hitting the deck above. As the man turned, puzzled, his face was clearly visible in the glowing dashboard lights.

It was Richard Livingstone.

With narrowed eyes and a grim mouth, Richard leaned toward the plexiglass dome. Big wipers fought the lashing spray as the schooner moved from the shelter of the breakwater. Waves began to slam the *Quest,* making the oil lamp's yellow light sway crazily and the wooden hull groan. The marine radio crackled, but no messages were heard.

The outside door opened.

Down the stairs came a woman in foul weather gear, wearing a navy watch cap. It was Kathy Munro. As she climbed up into the second bucket seat, Richard looked at her in surprise.

"Kathy! Was that you I just heard jump on deck from the breakwater?"

She nodded. "My car broke down, so I only just

reached the breakwater. Another 30 seconds, and the *Quest* would have sailed." She studied Richard's face. "Where are you bound, sweetheart?"

He shrugged. "Nowhere special. Just a little run to get some fresh air."

"Sure thing," Kathy said. She smiled. "You've got extra passengers. Who are they?"

Richard glanced at the Prince and his Emissary. "Oh, nobody important. Just a couple of stowaways."

Kathy laughed. "You're a rotten liar, Richard. I know who your prisoners are, and I know where you're going."

"You don't know anything."

"You've got the Ice Diamond lying on that bunk. He's worth twenty gold bars to the revolutionaries waiting on the yacht." Kathy smiled. "Still think I don't know anything?"

Richard scowled. "How'd you find out?"

"From you, at first. You once bragged about your grandfather having connections to foreign royalty. You said a king stayed at the place where your grandfather was born. When I read about the mystery prince in hiding, I wondered if he might be lying low where his ancestor once visited. I did some snooping in your office and saw the words Ice Diamond. It sounded like a code to me."

"Okay," Richard said. "So you've got a few brains. Tell you what, I'll give you a gold bar. That'll keep you quiet."

"I decided to find the Prince, and sell him myself," Kathy said. "BMWs cost a lot, you know. So I got some hired help from Alberta. On their way out on the plane, they heard the Austens talking about an Ice Diamond signal. I asked Tom and Liz some questions, and decided the yacht was outside Petty Harbour. I knew the Prince was somewhere nearby, probably at your grandfather's birthplace, so all I needed was the exact location."

Richard looked at her.

"By the time your thugs broke into my mansion I'd already destroyed the birth certificate. You took a real risk, Kathy. What if they'd been arrested? The cops would have traced them to you."

"Not a chance, Richard. You had a big secret to protect, so you'd never have called the police. You didn't want them snooping around, asking questions. Not when you'd sneaked the Prince and his Emissary into the country with a lie about representing the government. You planned to betray the Prince, and that was a secret you wanted to protect."

"The kids captured your thugs at my mansion. I suppose you're the one who secretly untied them."

"That's right."

"You know, when we first arrived at the mansion that night you made a mistake. You asked the Austens how the couple had got inside. You couldn't have known there were two of them, unless you were their boss. You also knew they'd blown up the safe."

Kathy smiled. "Sure, but nobody noticed the mistake. Same thing when I told you to use the cellular phone to call the cops. How'd I already know the phone lines were dead? Only because I'd ordered my people to cut them."

"I think you used me, Kathy, to find the Prince. You'd have sold him, and taken all the gold bars for yourself."

"You're right, Richard. I was never going to marry you, with the way you use people and your bad attitude towards women. I just pretended to love you, so I could use you to find the Prince."

"You're a betrayer, Kathy. That's terrible."

"Haven't you betrayed the Prince and his Emissary?"

Ignoring her, Richard said, "Did you send your thugs into the church at Petty Harbour?"

"Sure thing, Sweetheart. When I arrived at the *Quest* with Dave Foster, I heard the Austens talking about checking birth records at the church. That's what gave me the idea."

"I got to the church first," Richard said, "and ripped out the page. I thought I had already destroyed everything that gave my grandfather's birth place, but I'd forgotten the church."

"Well," Kathy said, "it's all been fun. I've enjoyed our times together on the *Quest,* Richard. Those twenty gold bars should buy me a nice little boat for my leisure hours."

"Twenty gold bars? You're getting exactly one." Richard studied the night, then he turned to Kathy and gasped. "That's a gun you're holding."

She nodded. "You bet. All the gold bars are mine. Get the picture, sweetheart? All of them."

10

For several minutes Richard was silent. Finally he looked at Kathy with hurt eyes. "How could you betray me?"

"This isn't betrayal, Richard. This is called being smart. Once you had those gold bars you'd be long gone, fella. I know your type."

"Lies." Richard tightened his grip on the wheel, glanced at the gun in Kathy's hand, then looked out at the sea. "What happened to your thugs tonight?" he said cynically. "I don't see them here."

"I guess something went wrong. When I heard Mrs. Chalmers and the kids figure out where the Prince was hiding, I called their cellular phone. My people were supposed to kidnap the Prince and bring him to the *Quest*.

We planned to overpower you, and use the schooner to reach the yacht. But I've switched to my fall-back plan, and it's working nicely. I'll still get rich, but I won't have to pay those two. Anyway, they won't need money in prison."

"There's the flare!" The brass on the wheel glowed, and Richard and Kathy's faces turned crimson in the sudden light from outside. As Henry squawked in his cage, Richard grabbed his binoculars to study the night. "The yacht's straight ahead."

Kathy motioned with the gun. "You'd better use the outside controls. Bring the megaphone on deck."

As the door closed behind them, Tom and Liz sprang out of hiding. Liz glanced at the hostages, who were still out cold, then pointed at the leather bucket seats.

"Let's watch from there."

Crawling into the seats, Tom and Liz looked out of the bubble. Directly ahead was the long, sleek yacht, rolling and pitching in the big waves. Lights along the deck shone on white steel, brass bells and mahogany doors. As a signal light flashed from the bridge, people on deck watched Richard use the outside controls to bring the schooner closer.

"Attention," called Richard's voice, made huge by the electronic megaphone. "We have the Ice Diamond on board. Do you have the gold bars?"

"Yes," cried a magnified voice from the bridge high above on the yacht. "But we want proof the Prince is with you."

"How do we know you've got the gold bars?"

"Come aboard. We will show the gold. But bring proof the Prince is with you."

Tom motioned at the barrels. "Let's hide! He may come below."

Moments later, the outside door opened. Tom and Liz

heard the whistle of the wind and the surging waves, then Richard coming down the stairs. "I hope the Prince brought those identity cards I faked for him," he muttered to himself. He was silent, searching, then said, "Ah! Thank goodness, here's his photo ID. That's perfect."

The door closed as he went outside, and Tom and Liz rushed to the bucket seats. Heavy seas tossed the vessels as they moved closer together. Stairs were lowered down the side of the yacht and lines were tossed to the schooner. With the two vessels together, Kathy and Richard leapt onto the landing stairs, climbed them, and disappeared inside the yacht.

"Quick," Liz said. "Let's throw off the lines, and make a fast trip back to Petty Harbour."

"I'll bring the binoculars, in case we need them."

Out on deck, they separated. Liz struggled across the heaving deck toward the bow, and Tom staggered to the stern. The wet lines were only looped in place, so it wasn't difficult to get them loose. As the ropes dropped away freeing the *Quest* from the yacht, a voice shouted from the bridge.

"Two people on the schooner! Get them!"

Tom and Liz scrambled to the outside helm. "Grab the wheel," Tom yelled. "I'll keep watch with the binoculars."

Liz gunned the engine and the schooner moved away from the yacht, as Tom scanned it with his binoculars. "They've started hauling up their anchor!"

Liz fed the engine maximum RPMs. The schooner surged over a breaking wave, then plowed down into the wild seas before rising high again. Above, the wind shrieked in the rigging as waves burst over the hull and foamed across the deck.

"I can see the house lights at Petty Harbour," Liz yelled, "but where's the notch in the breakwater? We're moving fast, and I've got to put this thing straight through it."

"I'll radio Duncan!" Tom shouted.

Down the cabin steps, he raced to the bubble. Finding Duncan's frequency, he grabbed the microphone. "Mayday, Mayday!" With the binoculars Tom studied the yacht behind. Seawater streamed from the anchor as it rose to the deck, and the big vessel began to move.

"They're coming after us!"

Duncan's voice crackled from the radio. "Tom? I'm here with Sarah. What's happening?"

Quickly they discussed strategy, then Tom signed off and rushed on deck. Sea spray lashed the schooner, making him grab a handhold as the *Quest* rolled deeply onto its side. Then, once more, they were racing toward the lights of Petty Harbour. Liz gained valuable seconds on the yacht, but it was still close behind.

Tom grabbed the binoculars. "The plan's working," he shouted, studying the breakwater. "Hang in there, Liz! In seconds you'll know where the notch is!"

Through the binoculars, Tom watched people rushing toward the breakwater from their homes. With them was Ginger Watson. Hurrying to the notch in the middle of the breakwater, she switched on a flashlight. Across the notch, someone clicked on another one. Then more flashlights began to glare, all along the breakwater.

"Fantastic," Liz shouted. "That pattern of lights shows me exactly where the notch is!"

Tom looked back. The yacht, driven by its power, was closing in fast. Ahead, the sea roared against a low reef, throwing white water into the dark night. As the *Quest* plunged toward the danger, Liz fought the wheel hard to starboard. The schooner rose high on a wave, bending under the wind, then finally changed direction and raced safely past the reef.

Now the breakwater was straight ahead. For a moment they saw the faces of the people holding the flashlights, then the Quest ran straight through the notch into the harbour's safety. As Tom and Liz braced themselves, the hull scraped loudly along the shallow harbour bottom and the schooner shuddered to a stop.

Rowboats immediately pulled away from wharfs, bringing help. Tom and Liz saw their cousins on the deck of their boat, then looked at the breakwater where the people were running to shelter.

"The flashlights are gone!" Tom looked out to sea. "They won't know where the breakwater is!"

Out of the night came the yacht. It looked big and powerful, but several helpless cries were heard from on board. Water curved away from the sleek white hull as the yacht ran in from sea, then slammed straight into the concrete and wood of the breakwater. For long seconds the night shook with the noise of the collision, then all was silent, except for the barking of dogs.

People scrambled off the yacht, jumping to the breakwater where they were seized by some big fishermen who had come running. Somewhere below deck on the yacht, there was a rumbling sound, followed by the belching of black smoke from the funnel and open doors. Everyone ran for cover. Seconds later, the glass of windows and portholes exploded out. Wood and steel blew apart, and the night turned into fire as the yacht exploded.

*   *   *

Two days later, Petty Harbour was still vibrating with excitement. The media had visited, bringing cameras and microphones, and everyone had been interviewed.

Tom and Duncan were on the porch outside the house.

It was night, and snow would soon fall from the dark skies. The cousins were waiting for it. With them was Tom's father, who had been telling the boys his feelings about Nanny.

"Brrr," Mr. Austen said at last. "It's cold out. In Arizona I got used to the sun, so I'll go inside now."

"See you later, Dad," Tom said. "It's great to have you here at last."

A few minutes later, headlights appeared in the village below. Twisting past houses, a car came up the hill and stopped. "That's a Mercedes," Tom said. "Look at those lines. I bet that guy just came from the airport."

"How'd you know . . . ?"

Duncan was interrupted by a man who'd stepped out of the car. He was young, handsome and blond. "Excuse me, I'm looking for Duncan and Sarah Joy, and Tom and Liz Austen. Is this the house?"

"Yup," Duncan replied, introducing himself and Tom.

"I just flew in from Toronto," the man said. "I rented this car and drove straight down."

Duncan turned to Tom. "You must be psychic!"

He laughed. "No, I just know that Mercedes is a German company, and there's a Tilden sticker on the window. They've got a special at the airport on those imports."

"You know," the man said, "you two and the girls did a great job and I've come to thank you myself. Richard Livingstone will be spending a long time in prison, and I'm happy about that."

"I recognize your face from somewhere," Tom said. "Are you a TV reporter or something?"

The man shook his head. "No, I'm Richard Livingstone the Fourth.

As the boys stared at him in astonishment, a loud cry

sounded from the Mercedes. The man reached into the back seat and opened the door of a brass cage. In a moment, Henry was on his shoulder. His feathers shone splendidly in the light from the windows, and his voice was loud.

The man grinned. "I think Henry's happy that I'm home."

Duncan nodded. "He looks great."

"Call me Richard Four, by the way. All my friends do." He looked up at the dark sky. "The air here smells good when snow's coming. Say, you kids are something else! I hear the police have just captured the bounty hunters who worked for my father, and they've also arrested Kathy's two people."

Tom nodded. "The Renegades were still tangled inside those nets when the police reached the tunnel."

"Listen," the man said, "don't be surprised that I'm glad my father's in trouble. He's bullied people all his life, thinking he was a big shot when secretly he was a coward and a betrayer. He lied when he told the Emissary and the Prince that he was their contact person for the government, and he had them kidnapped. Now he's been caught, so it's only fair that he serve his punishment. I still hope he'll change, but my great-grandfather really did a number on him."

"What do you mean?" Tom asked.

"People around here called him Old Man Livingstone, maybe because his attitudes were out of the Dark Ages. He raised my father from a child, and Dad never had a chance. He became as greedy and ruthless as the old guy."

"That's kind of sad," Duncan said.

The man nodded. "I've come home to take over Livingstone Sea Profits, so things at the company will now be different. I'm cancelling the park, and the tenants can stay. Instead of a park I'll build state-of-the-art playgrounds for their kids, and a community hall where people can be together. Won't that be neat?"

The house door opened, and Ginger Watson came out. She looked at the man, then grinned. "Richard Four! You've come home at last. Times are tough these days, Richard. We'll be needing your help, boy."

"You've got it." Going inside, he paused to look at Tom and Duncan. "My father resented women for wanting their fair share of life. I heard him grumble about it plenty of times." He grinned. "Well, guess what? Livingstone Sea Profits has a new Chief Executive Officer. She's great, and I'm about to hire some other talented women for my company. We'll do really well now!"

Tom smiled. "My Mom's sure going to be happy to hear that news. I think Nanny would have been, too." As the door closed behind Richard Four, Tom looked up at the sky. "Still no snow, and I'm cold."

"Let's see what's happening inside."

Lots of people were visiting, and a party had started. History Fred stood on a chair, capturing Mrs. Chalmers and Aunt Millie on video as they danced a reel in the middle of the big kitchen. Mr. Joy was on the accordion, and Aunt Lesley had her guitar. As people sang along, an elderly man used a couple of spoons to make amazing rhythms while his wife played the harmonica.

Richard Livingstone the Fourth smiled in a corner, clapping in time to the music. On his shoulder Henry bounced around, then began to sing. "That's Memories," Richard laughed. "I taught that song to Henry when I was a teenager."

"Richard Four," Ginger called across the kitchen.

"How are you feeling, boy?"

"Happy to be home, Ginger. It feels grand."

*   *   *

In the TV room, Liz cuddled baby Samantha as her cousin put on a video. A screen glowed, and they saw the Prince's handsome face. Flapping behind him were the flags of Newfoundland, Canada and the Prince's own country. "I announce my claim to the throne," he said. "I will take this matter to the World Court."

"He's so self-confident," Sarah said. "He'll make a wonderful King. I wonder who'll share his throne? I'd better stay in touch."

"Don't forget we're planning to explore Europe together. Don't fall in love until after that."

"I'll try," Sarah said, "but I can't promise."

On the screen, the Prince continued to speak. "I wish to salute the people of Canada for their love of peace." He smiled at his Emissary, who stood nearby. "We will never forget Newfoundland."

"Fast forward to where he thanks us," Sarah said. "That's my favourite part."

There was a knock, and Mr. Austen came into the room. The Arizona sun had tanned his skin, and he looked relaxed in jeans and a checked shirt. "I missed all the excitement around here. You kids did well." He picked up a book from Sarah's desk. "Hey, a copy of *Silent Spring*. I read this when I was your age, Sarah. This book started people caring about the environment."

Sarah nodded. "I'm researching a report for school on Earth Day, Uncle Ted."

"That's great, because now your generation is leading the fight to save our planet." Mr. Austen smiled. "I'm proud of you. I know the future's in strong hands."

*   *   *

Outside the house, soft flakes drifted down from the sky. Tom and Duncan caught the liquid stars on their tongues, then walked down the hill to the harbour. All over the village lights were on, warming the night.

"Pretty soon the breakwater will be repaired," Duncan said. "I'm glad you got some pictures of the wrecked yacht."

"Remember when I radioed from the schooner, saying Liz couldn't see the breakwater? That was a great idea of yours, having people shine their flashlights from it."

"Thanks," Duncan said proudly.

"You know that night we climbed Spyglass Hill? We saw Richard on the schooner, looking out to sea. The signal was for him. He was going to sell the Prince to pay off his debts and build Livingstone Park. It might have made the *Guiness Book of Records* as the biggest monument ever to an ego." Tom held his face up to the falling snow. "Know a clue I missed when we met Kathy at her office? She asked about the Ice Diamond, but that was a police secret. She already knew the code word, and had told the Renegades. That's why they wanted to know where you'd seen the signal flashing to shore."

Duncan watched the falling snow settle softly on rooftops and porches, boats and wharfs. The night was still and quiet. "There'll be lots of people cooling their heels in prison after this little caper. Remember when we saw the Renegades' Jeep on that side road? I guess they were meeting Kathy inside the BMW."

Tom nodded. "Know what should have tipped me? BMWs are made in Germany, and I'd seen a picture in her office of the German town where she got her car."

"What about POWER on her licence plate?"

Tom smiled. "That didn't mean anything. It just kept us from concentrating on the BMW being the clue. But I guess POWER was Kathy's goal — she just needed a lot of money first."

"Remember after the funeral when Mrs. Chalmers helped us figure out both the secret meaning of Ice Diamond and where the Prince was hiding? Kathy was also was on the porch, listening."

Tom nodded. "Then she went inside and called the Renegades' cellular phone. We heard that woman being told about the lighthouse, but only Kathy had that information."

"And Mrs. Chalmers."

"She's not the criminal type."

"But she's right out of the pages of Agatha Christie! I thought you read her mysteries. On the train, when you . . . ."

Tom smiled. "Of course I do. But I still trust Mrs. Chalmers."

"Maybe you're right." Duncan sighed. "I've got to find another mystery somewhere. After all that's happened, the Harbour's going to seem pretty quiet." He glanced up at his cousin. His eyes were shy. "Say, Tom, I've been thinking."

"What about?"

"Well, I . . . . You know, I was . . . wondering. Do you suppose all this might be in a book some day?"

Tom grinned. "I think the chances are pretty good."

Author photo by Dale Wilson

About the Author

One thing Eric Wilson likes best about being an author is exploring Canada, so he enjoyed discovering St. John's and Petty Harbour in November. Although this book is fiction, some events in the plot were inspired by stories told to Eric while he was in Newfoundland.

"If you're looking for material," he suggests to young writers, "talk to your family and your neighbours. Older people have lived stories that can curl you hair or warm your romantic heart! They're out there — just waiting to be told."

Have you joined

THE ERIC WILSON MYSTERY CLUB

????

It's exciting, and it's all FREE!

Here's what you'll receive:
~ a membership card
~ a regular newsletter
~ a chance to win books
personally autographed by
Eric Wilson

It's FREE, so just send your name, date of birth,
home address with town and postal code to:

The Eric Wilson Mystery Club
Harper & Collins Publishers Ltd.
Suite 2900, Hazelton Lanes
55 Avenue Road
Toronto, Ontario
M5R 3L2

COLD MIDNIGHT IN VIEUX QUÉBEC
A Tom Austen Mystery

Eric Wilson

Fireworks exploded into the sky above the Ice palace as Tom struggled forward through the throngs of people, then was suddenly grabbed by a big police officer.

"Tu ne peux pas aller là-bas. *That is a security zone.*"

"*You've got to let me get past,*" *Tom shouted.*

The leaders of the world's superpowers have agreed to meet in Quebec City to put an end to chemical weapons — but powerful forces will stop at nothing to prevent the agreement from being signed. From the first chilling page, you will be gripped by suspense as you follow Tom Austen and Dietmar Oban through the ancient, mysterious streets of *Vieux Québec* in quest of world peace.

CODE RED AT THE SUPERMALL
A Tom and Liz Austen Mystery

Eric Wilson

They swam past gently-moving strands of sea-weed and pieces of jagged coral, then Tom almost choked in horror. A shark was coming straight at him, ready to strike.

Have you ever visited a shopping mall that has sharks and piranhas, a triple-loop rollercoaster, 22 waterslides, an Ice Palace, submarines, 828 stores, and a major mystery to solve? Soon after Tom and Liz Austen arrive at the West Edmonton Mall a bomber strikes and they must follow a trail that leads through the fabled spendours of the supermall to hidden danger.

THE GREEN GABLES DETECTIVES
A Liz Austen Mystery

Eric Wilson

*I almost expected to see Anne signalling to Diana
from her bedroom window as we climbed the
slope towards Green Gables, then Makiko
grabbed my arm. "Danger!"*

*Staring at the house, I saw a dim shape slip
around a corner into hiding. "Who's there?" I
called. "We see you!"*

While visiting the famous farmhouse known as
Green Gables, Liz Austen and her friends are
swept up in baffling events that lead from an
ancient cemetery to a haunted church, and then
a heart-stopping showdown in a deserted lighthouse as fog swirls across Prince Edward Island.
Be prepared for eerie events and unbearable suspense as you join the Green Gables detectives for
a thrilling adventure.